COWGIRL UNDERCOVER

QUEENS OF MONTANA, BOOK 3

VANESSA GRAY BARTAL

DRY CREEK PRESS

CHAPTER 1

If I don't get out of this house I'm going to scream, Kitty thought. Love was in the air, and it was suffocating her. In a few short weeks, her sister, Libby, was getting married to their ranch foreman, Dobbie. After that her oldest sister, Anne, was marrying her longtime boyfriend, Will. Both men had proposed the previous summer. Will and Libby had pushed for a double wedding, to which Anne and Dobbie had each replied, "Over my dead body."

Now Libby was getting the wedding of her dreams in their church, and Anne was getting her desired ceremony in the horse barn. Dobbie and Will had given their brides carte blanche to do what they wanted with one stipulation: Dobbie told Libby she had to take a honeymoon and wasn't allowed to work herself into a frenzy before she got there, and Will told Anne she had to wear a dress. Little did he know she would be wearing her mother's wedding gown.

The two engaged couples weren't Kitty's problem. She loved both her future brothers-in-law like family already, and she was happy her sisters were marrying them. No, her problem came from another source—her sixteen year old little sister, Maggie. She was perfect. Besides being exquisitely beautiful, she was terminally sweet and good; she never had a bad thought or word about anyone. Sarcasm wasn't in her repertoire, and she couldn't understand it on the rare occasions Kitty used it on her. Kitty could overlook those glaring flaws if not for one important thing: Mathew Henshaw.

Mathew was her age, eighteen. For as long as they had been neighbors, Kitty had been in love with him. And for as long as she could remember, Mathew had been in love with Maggie. And for as long as Mathew had been in love with Maggie, she had been oblivious to him.

At least she was safe in the knowledge that no one knew of her feelings. She had never told a living soul: not her sisters, not her best friend Cecily, and certainly not Mathew himself. Thoughts of him, or anyone, finding out filled her with mortification. As long as she kept her distance from him she was safe, but now that he had graduated from high school, it was impossible. He showed up at their house every day riding his beautiful stallion. And every day he tipped his Stetson to her and said, "Kitty," in a polite, disinterested way before dismounting to find the true object of his desire: Maggie. More often than not he brought Maggie a present, like a cute field mouse he had captured, or an interesting snake skin he had found. She had to give him credit; he knew her animal-loving sister well.

She always buried her face in a book and lost herself in fictional worlds whenever he arrived. Lately she had been dwelling on Jane Austen, but it was making her melancholy. Where were the Mr. Darcys of the world when she needed them?

The sound of hooves pounding interrupted her reverie, and she snapped to attention as Mathew streaked into the yard.

"Kitty," he said in his perfect voice and tipped his perfect hat. Absently she wondered how he was able to keep the hat free of dirt when he rode through a half hour of dust to get here, but it was one more sign of his faultlessness. He was almost mythical, she thought, from his tawny blond hair and crystal blue eyes, to his tall handsome physique.

"Mathew," she replied, hoping her voice didn't sound as breathless to him as it did to her.

"Where's your sister?" he asked as he dismounted. His perfect horse would stand in that spot until he was told to do otherwise.

"Which one?" she asked.

"Funny."

Maggie exited the house and Mathew's face changed from amusement to rapture. "Hey, baby girl."

"Hey, Mathew," Maggie said cheerfully. In her world it was normal for handsome, wealthy young men to dote on her. What must that be like, Kitty wondered.

"I'm going to check my email," Kitty announced, but Mathew and Maggie were already deep in conversation. "And then I'm going to set my hair on fire," she added.

"Have fun," Mathew said absently, and without breaking eye contact with Maggie.

She let herself into the house and tried not to feel the pain of being ignored. It wasn't her sister's fault she was irresistible, and therefore it wasn't Mathew's fault he couldn't resist her. The logic that was usually her faithful friend did nothing to lift her spirits today.

She sat in front of her computer without seeing it. Some part of her brain registered her lack of emails. Why had she thought she would have any? She didn't know anyone besides her family and her neighbors. Thoughts of her neighbors reminded her to check her phone to see if her best friend and neighbor, Cecily, had called. Kitty didn't own a cell phone because their Montana ranch was too far away from a tower. Instead they had individual voicemail. She punched in her password and then sat up in alarm as Cecily's voice came on the line.

"Kitty, you have to help me." She sounded panicked and desperate. "They're sending me away. I don't know when I'll ever see you again. I'm scared." She whispered the last part, started to sob, and then the line went dead. Kitty called her back but no one answered. Their cook was always there. Was something truly wrong?

She went to the barn where the family truck was kept, and then found out Libby and Dobbie had taken it into town for their premarital counseling session with the pastor. Reluctantly she turned and saddled her horse. She didn't mind riding. She rather enjoyed it, but she was worried, and driving would have been more expedient.

As she rode, she thought. Cecily's parents were divorced. She and her father had lived alone with their cook until the last few months. Her father, Yancey Blake, had run for local political office. When his bid failed, he took up with a crowd of strangers who soon moved into their bunkhouse. Kitty's father, Matt Chapman, was suspicious of the strangers because of some comments he had overheard. He tried to broach the subject with Yancey, but had abruptly been told to mind his own business. Since then Yancey had become reclusive and secretive. Cecily was rarely allowed to visit Kitty, and Kitty had been so caught up in wedding plans and preparations that she hadn't visited Cecily in weeks.

She was lost in thought as she approached the Blake's long lane, so it took her a moment to realize she was being flagged down. In fact, she didn't realize it until a man grabbed her horse's reins and she saw his gun.

"You're going to have to turn around, Ma'am," he said. Despite the fact he had called her ma'am, his tone wasn't polite.

"Excuse me?" she asked.

"You heard me," he said coldly. He was a large, burly man with bulging biceps. It was redundant for him to be holding a rifle when he could break her with his bare hands.

"What gives you the right to deny me access to my neighbor's land?" she asked.

"Mr. Blake specified no visitors," the man said.

"I'm here to visit his daughter Cecily," Kitty tried. Maybe it was the nature of Montana, but she was used to muscled men with guns and remained unintimidated by this stranger.

"She's not here," he said.

"Where has she gone?" Kitty asked.

"Not my business."

Something was very, very wrong here. She studied the man as she tried to decide what to do. Obviously he wasn't going to allow her to pass. She would have to circumvent him. She gave him a curt nod and turned her horse toward home. As soon as she was sure she was out of his sight, she dismounted.

She pulled a piece of paper and pen from her bag and wrote a note telling her family she would be home later. She pinned it to her horse's blanket, told him to go home, and slapped his rump. She watched him go with some trepidation. The long walk home was going to be dark, but it couldn't be helped. Cecily and her father may be in trouble, and it was her duty as their neighbor to help if she could.

She turned back toward the Blakes' spread with a flutter of nervous excitement in her chest. When she and Cecily were little girls, they had spent their childhoods exploring the paths around both their houses. Now was the time to put that knowledge to use. She pulled her socks up over her pant legs to avoid ticks and set off through the tall grass. Fortunately she knew which pastures were for the bulls and which were for the cows. She hopped the fence of a cow pasture, glad for the cover they provided. She stopped at the fence closest to the house and looked around to make sure no one was in sight.

There were two men, but they had their backs to her, and they were carrying guns. She vaulted the fence and stealthily made her way toward the house.

Once she reached the barn, she crept inside. She was almost at the exit on the other side when hands grabbed her and threw her down onto the hay. A body landed gently on top of her. A man pressed two fingers of his left hand to her lips and the index finger of his right hand to his own lips. She opened her mouth to scream, but then she heard them.

"Are you sure you saw someone?" one man asked.

"I thought I did," a second man said.

"Probably an animal," the first man said. "Place is crawling with them. Makes me nervous."

The other man grunted, and she heard feet shuffling as if they were leaving. The man on top of her kept his fingers pressed to her lips until he was sure they were gone. When he moved his fingers she opened her mouth to speak, but he covered it with his own and kissed her passionately.

After a moment of shock, she recovered enough to draw her head back from his, and then she slapped him hard across the face. He massaged the area where she had hit and smiled before opening his mouth to speak.

"Nice to see you, too, Kat."

CHAPTER 2

Kitty gasped. There was only one person on earth who ever called her Kat.

"Dante," she exclaimed.

"One and the same," he said. He rolled off and stretched out beside her, keeping his palm pressed flat against her stomach.

"I haven't seen you in…"

"Six years," he finished for her. Dante was Cecily's older brother. He was two years older and had moved to Chicago with his mother when their parents divorced. To her knowledge, he hadn't been back since.

"What are you doing here?" she asked.

"Spending some quality time with my father. What are you doing here?"

"Checking on Cecily. I received a near hysterical message from her."

"My sister lives her life in a state of near hysteria. I'm surprised you responded, knowing her the way you do."

"She said she was being sent away," Kitty said.

"That's true," Dante said.

"Who sent her?"

"I did."

"Why?"

He smiled indulgently at her. "Always inquisitive, aren't you, Kat? She needed to spend some time with our mom."

"And it has nothing to do with the men walking around here carrying guns?" Kitty asked.

He shrugged and looked away.

"Dante, what's going on?"

"Nothing. Dad has some new friends, and they're a little paranoid." He still wouldn't meet her eyes.

"Paranoid is locking your doors at night when the only danger around here is a rogue grizzly. Carrying AK47's and denying your neighbors entrance is all out crazy."

He twirled his index finger in a lock of her long, chestnut colored hair. "You grew up gorgeous, Kat."

"You're being hyperbolic," she said. "And you're changing the subject."

He chuckled. "Good to know you've only changed on the outside. We were both going through an awkward stage last time we were together."

That was certainly true. She'd had short, frizzy hair, braces, glasses, and a bad complexion. Dante had been her height, which was short for a boy. He was chubby, painfully shy, and awkward at sports.

His father had made no secret of the fact that his son was a disappointment to him. He picked on him incessantly and unabashedly favored Cecily. It was one of the main reasons for their parents' divorce, and it was why Dante had left with his mother and not returned.

She studied him now. She was five-six, and he was a good six inches taller than her, well built with dark brown hair, dark eyes, and a dark complexion. His mother was of Spanish descent, and he had her coloration.

"What's going on with the Chapman clan?" he asked. He was watching her intently, and he seemed amused by her inspection of him.

"Libby and Anne are getting married this summer."

"What about Maggie?" he asked.

"Maggie's fine," she said.

"Uh-oh, are you and Maggie fighting?"

She was surprised by his perception. She thought she masked any negativity in her tone. "No, we're not fighting. Maggie is as sweet and guileless as ever."

"Hmm." He eyed her suspiciously.

"What's up with you?" she asked.

"I'll be a junior this year at Northwestern."

"Do you like Chicago?" she asked.

"It's okay."

"What's your major?"

"Math."

She whistled. "Smarty."

He smiled. "Look who's talking. If you attended high school you would have been the valedictorian."

"Did you attend high school?" she asked. She had to homeschool because she was too far from the nearest high school to attend, but she loved school and was fascinated by anyone who went.

"I did." He looked away from her again.

"You're being secretive."

"You haven't seen me in six years. How do you know this isn't my normal personality?" He used the tendril of her hair he was holding to tickle her nose.

She wrinkled her nose and batted his hand away. "There are certain physiological signs of lying that aren't dependent on personality."

He blinked at her for a minute and burst out laughing. "Oh, Kat. I forgot how you are."

"What do you mean, how I am?"

"I forgot how you know everything about everything, and you don't speak with any emotion."

Her frown deepened into a scowl. "I don't know everything, and I have plenty of emotion."

His eyebrows arched. "Really? Could have fooled me the way you broke off our kiss like my lips were poison."

Kitty was beginning to truly dislike this new Dante. The boy she had known was sweet and agreeable. "I broke off the kiss because I had no idea who you were. You could have been a psychotic creep. Maybe you still are; I haven't decided."

"You really didn't recognize me? I knew you the minute I saw you hop the fence on the far pasture. Which, by the way, wasn't very smart."

"Why?" she asked in mock innocence. She wanted to make him admit there was something nefarious going on.

"Because you've never been the best athlete. I held my breath every time I saw you scale a fence."

Her mouth fell open slightly. The old Dante had followed her around almost worshipfully, like a puppy. This one insulted her, and she felt somewhat betrayed. "I handled the fences fine, thank you very much."

"And then you almost got caught," he added as if she hadn't spoken.

"By whom?" She batted her lashes at him.

"You have pretty eyes," he said. He ran a light finger over her lashes. "Such an interesting combination of brown and green."

She almost growled in frustration. "Dante, you're avoiding my questions. Who are those men? Why are they carrying guns? What is going on here?"

"Hadn't I better get you home?" he asked, and this time he was the one feigning innocence. They stared at each other in a standoff, and she crossed her arms over her chest.

"If you think I'm giving up this easily you don't remember me very well," she said. "We're in the middle of nowhere Montana, and now that you've sent my best friend away I have nothing better to do than try to figure out what's going on here." In truth she didn't care what was happening at the ranch. Generally she minded her own business, but Dante's obvious attempts to dodge her questions piqued her curiosity and frustrated her all at the same time. She would solve the mystery if only to show him she could do it.

He smiled at her in an amused, patronizing way that set her teeth on edge. When he reached his hand up to pat her head, her control snapped, and she bit him.

Quickly he withdrew his hand and then looked at it in amazement. "You bit me."

She didn't respond. She hadn't meant to bite him, but she wasn't about to apologize.

"You broke the skin." He held up his hand for her inspection.

There were four teeth marks in his hand, and little red spots appeared at each one. "I don't like to be touched without permission," she said by way of an explanation. It was probably the truth, but she had never tested the theory before because no one ever touched her. She thought of all the hugs Mathew and Maggie shared, and wondered if she was lying.

Dante was looking at her warily now. "I'll keep that in mind." He stood and held out a hand to her, but then snatched it back. "You're not going to wound me again, are you?"

She suppressed a smile. "You never know." She stood without his assistance and dusted herself off. "How are you going to get past the guard at the gate?"

"I'm not," Dante said. He led her to a stall, and she waited while he saddled his horse.

"Where's mine?" she asked.

"Your what?"

"My horse."

"You're riding with me," he said. She frowned. He sighed. "I am not leading a horse home when we can easily share my saddle. I don't remember you being this afraid of being touched before. We've danced together a few times, and you hugged me goodbye when I left. Did something happen to you?" He studied her with a concerned expression, and she had to admit she was touched.

"No." She looked away. Something had happened to *him*. Before he had been Dante, the chubby, gawky big brother of her best friend. Hugging him then had been like hugging the Pillsbury Doughboy. Now he was Dante, the handsome and self assured stranger she knew nothing about. She wasn't used to being around men in this way, and she was uncomfortable. Her vulnerability and discomfort were making her irritable, but she didn't want to make any more a fool of herself than she already had; so when he was firmly settled in the saddle, she swung up in front of him.

"You smell good," he said. He leaned forward slightly and put his face near her neck.

"Stop sniffing me."

"You have a lot of rules, Kat."

"It tickles," she said, barely loud enough for him to hear. The fact that she was incredibly ticklish was only known by a handful of people, and she wanted to keep it that way. Being ticklish seemed beneath her somehow.

"Oh," he said, and she could tell he was smiling.

They were quiet for a few minutes until they reached the end of the lane. The guard who had so rudely sent her away glared at her as they approached.

"How'd you get in?" he asked.

She didn't answer him.

"She is welcome here anytime," Dante said, and Kitty was amazed by the tone of cool authority in his voice.

"The boss won't like this."

"Then he can take it up with me. Miss Chapman is our friend and neighbor, and I expect you to let her enter in the future. Is that understood?"

Kitty could feel the man chafing under Dante's instruction, but finally he gave a curt nod, and they were on their way again.

"Why is your father keeping everyone away from the ranch?" she asked.

"He isn't. He let me in," he said, and sounded amused.

"But not me," she said.

"He would have, if he had known. Some of the newcomers are a little over-zealous. You were right about the boredom of Montana. They need something to do with their time, and some of them like to pretend they're in special forces or something."

That made no sense. They had plenty of ranch hands, and they were busy from sunup to sundown. There was always work to be done, and never enough time in the day. They liked to have fun, but they were never stuck for ways to find it. How did these new cowboys suddenly have so much time that they were looking for things to do? She was distracted from her thoughts when Dante spoke.

"So Anne and Dobbie are finally getting married?"

"No, Anne is marrying Will. Libby is marrying Dobbie."

"Who is Will?" he asked.

"He was our tutor a few years ago. Anne moved with him to Pittsburgh. She graduated college and is getting ready to start law school there."

"Wait, back up the train. Anne left the ranch?"

"I know," she said. "We were all shocked."

"And poor Libby got stuck with Dobbie," he said.

She stiffened. "What's wrong with Dobbie?" Dobbie had lived with them since she was ten years old, and she counted him as a brother.

"What isn't wrong with Dobbie?" There was so much vehemence in his tone she turned in the saddle to look at him. She didn't say anything; she waited for him to speak. Finally he did, but it looked like he was having a difficult time controlling his emotions.

"My Dad loves Dobbie, okay? He's everything he ever wanted in a son: strong, athletic, and an amazing rancher. He was the son of his dreams."

She laid a gentle hand in his shoulder and he started. "Dante, you can't think your dad would actually prefer Dobbie to you."

"Oh, but he does. I heard him say it. When Dobbie's parents died, my dad wanted to take him in. He told my mom it would be nice to have a real man as a son, for once. My mom put her foot down. I think it was the last straw before their breakup."

She laid her other hand on his shoulder. Her twisted position in the saddle was awkward, but she felt compelled to offer comfort to her onetime friend. "I'm sorry," she said sincerely. "Your dad never knew what he was missing out on with you."

He swallowed hard. "Thanks, Kat." He smiled at her.

She smiled in return and faced forward again. "You realize it's not rational to take out your problems with your dad on Dobbie. He had no idea any of this was going on."

"Let me have my anger; I need it," he said. His tone was cryptic, but she knew if she asked him about it he wouldn't answer. "But I'll try not to direct it at Dobbie."

"You probably won't recognize him. He's so head-over-heels in love with Libby he doesn't even act like the same person."

"This I want to see," he said. "Speaking of which, why don't we hang out tomorrow?"

She hesitated. She wasn't sure she liked Dante as he was now, and she didn't know if she wanted to spend more time trying to find out.

"Come on," he coaxed. "With Cecily gone, I'm all alone. I need the moral support and the boredom relief."

"Sadly, being used as a boredom reliever isn't even the worst offer I've ever had," she said.

"You know what I mean," he said. "We used to be friends. We can be again. I promise I won't touch you. Unless you ask me to." He put his hand around her waist and drew her back against his chest. The physical sensation wasn't unpleasant, but she was annoyed he kept taking without asking, so she sat up and held herself stiffly away from him.

"Brr, it's cold out here," he said. "I don't usually get this many complaints."

"I don't usually complain," she said coolly. Of course, no one had ever tried anything on her, but maybe she wouldn't complain if it ever did happen.

"Touché," he said, and they rode the rest of the way to her house in silence.

CHAPTER 3

When they arrived at her house, Dobbie and Libby were in the barn. They looked up from their embrace as Dante and Kitty approached. At the sight of Dobbie, Dante tensed, and Kitty felt compelled to touch his forearm in a soothing gesture. He relaxed and caught her hand before she shook him off.

Dobbie and Libby wore matching curious expressions as first Kitty, and then Dante descended the horse. Strangers were a rare sight in these parts.

"Dante," Kitty said, and jerked her head toward him.

"Oh, my, you've changed." Libby blurted it before she could stop herself, gave an embarrassed chuckle, and hugged Dante. "It's nice to see you. Welcome home."

He smiled warmly and returned her hug. "Thanks, Libby. You look exactly like you did when we were in school. Still wearing those pretty dresses." They were the same age, and Kitty had never thought about the fact that they were in the same class when they were in school together.

Dobbie stepped forward and settled his arm securely around Libby in a not-so-subtle *she's taken* gesture. He held out his hand for Dante to shake.

"Good to see you, Blake," he said affably.

"You, too," Dante said, and Kitty wondered if her sister and Dobbie could hear the choked, strained quality in his tone. At least he was trying. She thought of the horrible way his father had treated him. Why? Why had he been so cruel to his sweet, sensitive son? Dante had turned out well despite his criticism and disinterest. Or had he? She studied him with narrowed eyes. She knew nothing about him now, and that was disconcerting. He caught her staring and turned to wink at her, an action which did not go unnoticed by their audience.

Libby cleared her throat. "Would you like to come in for a snack?"

"Sure," he said easily. He turned to fall in line with Kitty behind the other couple. When they reached the house, he stood in the entryway and inhaled.

"Would you believe I remember the scent of your house as well as my own? I wonder why that is." He shook his head.

Kitty wondered, too. He had occasionally accompanied Cecily on her visits, but not frequently. Mostly she saw him when she went to the Blakes' house, and then he and Cecily ended up arguing because she wanted him to leave them alone.

"Go play by yourself, Dante," she would yell. But then Kitty would see the hurt, lonely look on his face and insist he play with them, which only increased Cecily's fury. *"Sometimes I think you like my brother more than you like me,"* she would say. And sometimes she was right. Cecily was spoiled from all the attention her father lavished on her, and occasionally she could be demanding and self-centered; plus she was flighty and an airhead. Dante was thoughtful, caring, and down to earth. Cecily always wanted to play house or babies. Kitty and Dante preferred putting on plays, reading stories, or looking outside for interesting leaves and flowers. Cecily chattered relentlessly, but Dante was comfortable to sit silently side by side while he and Kitty did separate activities. Kitty loved Cecily and would never admit it, but sometimes Dante had been a relief from the hyper swirl of activity that surrounded her friend.

"Are you in there, Kat?" Dante asked, and her mind snapped back to the present.

"I'm sorry, what?" she said.

"You're standing there staring off into space. I was wondering what you're thinking."

She blinked at him a few times to clear away her mental fog. "I was thinking about the past. About you."

"The past is best left forgotten where I'm concerned," he said and strolled past her into the kitchen.

She frowned as she followed him. She couldn't remember ever frowning so much in one night. Her face almost hurt from the exercise. Why wouldn't Dante want her to remember him? He had been awkward, as had she, but they had both outgrown that stage. Surely he couldn't be insecure about the boy he had been. Lots of kids went through a gawky growth spurt, but most of them got over it. Pictures of herself as a twelve year old weren't her favorite, but she didn't try to deny they ever happened.

"Libby, this food is delicious," Dante said. "Good thing you burn a lot of calories on the ranch, or you would get fat," he added to Dobbie. Kitty wondered if he threw that in to mollify Dobbie who was still hovering jealously over Libby. Her suspicions were confirmed when Dante looked at her and gave her a conspiratorial grin.

She smiled and felt something warm within her. For once she was the one with an inside joke. For so many years she had been the outsider in her family. At five foot six, she was the tallest sister. Her chestnut hair was darker and curlier than the other sisters, and her brown-green eyes were different than the other sisters who all had light brown eyes. She was an introvert who liked to read, and on more than one occasion she had felt like an outsider looking in. Anne had worked the ranch while Libby worked in the house and kept them all fed and clothed. They filled in as mother and father, and Maggie was the delight of everyone's life. And then there was Kitty. Having an inside joke with Dante was small, but it made her understand how ostracized she felt in her own family, and the realization made her sad.

She felt Dante's hand on her knee as he gave it a squeeze. She stiffened and almost wrenched away from his touch, but when she saw the sympathetic look of understanding on his face, she stayed put. Of all people, he knew how it felt to be an outsider in his own family, and on a much worse scale than anything she had ever experienced. Suddenly it felt very nice to have someone on her team, and her heart warmed with affection for him. Maybe it would be nice to spend some time getting reacquainted with him, especially in light of Cecily's absence. Who else was there? She smiled at him, but when she looked up, her smile fled. Dobbie and Libby were watching them with knowing, amused smiles on their faces.

Kitty's cheeks flushed, and she gently squirmed away from Dante so he could no longer reach her. She wasn't one of those girls for whom physical affection came easily, like Maggie. She could hug or kiss people as easily as breathing. Libby was like that, too. She was always lavishing hugs and kisses on Maggie and her. Kitty was more reserved like her oldest sister, Anne. She enjoyed being affectionate, but it didn't come naturally to her, and especially not with someone she hadn't seen in six years.

Conversation swirled around her, but she didn't feel compelled to join in. Her family knew she was reserved and didn't speak unless she had something to say. She had never been one for idle chit chat; although, it didn't bother her when other people talked, as long as they were people she loved. Dante asked Libby and Dobbie how they got together, and then he asked them about the wedding. Kitty smiled as she listened. They made it sound so easy, but she had been witness to their courtship, and they had their fair share of trials. Like Shakespeare said, "The course of true love never did run smooth," and these two were living proof. She felt some measure of hope that she, too, would one day find what they had, despite any obstacles she might have to overcome. She smiled wryly to herself. For her, the biggest barrier would be overcoming the obstacles she had placed in her own path. She was reserved and uncomfortable with romance, although she craved it deeply. Plus there was the man. He would have to be nearly perfect in order to compete with the true desire of her heart.

As if thinking of him had conjured him Mathew was standing at the base of the steps when Kitty led Dante outside. Maggie was there, too, standing on the step above him. Kitty had been so focused on Mathew that she hadn't noticed her sister, but Dante did.

"Maggie," he said, in an astonished sort of way. "How are you?"

"Dante?" she asked after a moment's hesitation. "Oh, my goodness." She leaped up into his arms and hugged him tightly.

"Look at you all grown up," he said. "You were only ten years old when I went away, and still in pigtails." He tugged lightly on her glorious hair. Kitty felt an odd stirring that was something like jealousy, and she wasn't the only one. Mathew cleared his throat.

"Hi, Dante," he said, and his voice held a slight challenge.

Dante smiled and let Maggie go. He held out his hand to Mathew. "Hello, Mathew." Was it Kitty's imagination, or was Dante's voice cool when he spoke to him? Surely he couldn't have fallen in love with Maggie so quickly that he already realized Mathew was his competition. Or could he? Maggie was beautiful, sweet, and affectionate. She repressed a sigh. Did all men everywhere fall in love with her sister on sight?

Mathew released Dante's hand and put his arm around Maggie, exactly the same as Dobbie had done earlier with Libby. To Kitty's surprise Dante reached out and did the same thing to *her*.

"Kat was walking me to my horse," Dante explained unnecessarily. "But I'll see you tomorrow."

"You will?" Kitty asked.

"Sure," he answered easily. "I can't stay away from my girl." He smiled and winked. At her. She knew this because she looked behind her to make sure there was no one else. He tugged her hand to lead her to the barn.

"What was that about?" she asked when they reached his horse.

"I got it," he said.

"You got what?" she asked irritably. She didn't like not knowing things. She was usually the sharpest tool in the shed, and the fact that she was missing out on something vital bugged her to no end.

"You like him."

She was glad it was dark because her face blushed crimson. "Who?" she asked weakly.

"Oh, come on, Kat. I would have to be blind not to notice. You lit up like a Roman candle as soon as we reached the porch."

"I did no such thing," she said.

"You did," he argued. "But don't worry; I'm going to help you out."

"What do you mean by that?" she asked. What she wanted most was to flee somewhere private and bury her face in her hands. No one had ever guessed her secret crush on Mathew before, and she didn't want anyone to know about it now. She was mortified.

"I know things about guys and girls, and dating. I'm sort of a master at this type of thing. You need to make him jealous, and I'm the guy to do it."

She scraped her teeth over her lip in a nervous gesture. "What are you talking about?" She was so far out of her element here; she didn't even have a reference point.

"I'm going to be your boyfriend," he said.

CHAPTER 4

"Huh?" She was talking like she had no intelligence, but she couldn't help it.

He smiled and touched his index finger to the tip of her nose. "Cute."

"Huh?" she repeated.

He let out a prolonged sigh. "You don't know much about men, do you?"

Her blush returned. "I've read all about the birds and the bees."

He laughed uncomfortably and then stifled it. "That wasn't what I was talking about, but that's good to know. Look, a guy doesn't want a girl when there is no competition for her. You're sitting here day after day, predictable and boring. If you're ever going to catch his interest or his eye, you've got to do something drastic."

"I don't want to catch his interest or his eye," she said, and lowered her voice. "He's Maggie's." She looked around furtively to make sure they were alone.

"Is he?" he asked. "She didn't seem interested in him at all."

"Well, she's not, but she will be someday, I'm sure. I mean, how could she not?"

"He's not that great."

Her eyebrows arched. "Are you in the market that you notice another guy's greatness?"

"I'm a competitor, as is he. I can guarantee you that at this very moment he is running me down to Maggie by pointing out all my flaws."

"Mathew wouldn't do that. He's a nice guy."

"He's a man, and all men are competitive for the girl they want. This is one of our tactics; we run other men down to make ourselves look better."

"Interesting," she said, and meant it. She loved learning new things. "What else can you tell me about men?"

"Only as much as I want you to know." He swung up into the saddle. "I'll see you tomorrow, Kat. We'll talk again."

She watched him go with an odd mixture of relief and reluctance, turned, and went into the house. And then wished she could immediately turn and go back out. Mathew, Maggie, Dobbie, and Libby were all in the living room, and it was obvious by the way they fell silent that they had been talking about her.

She froze with one foot dangling in midair. "Uh," she started, but didn't know how to continue.

"Dante has really changed," Libby said.

"Uh," Kitty said again.

"I didn't know he was coming home, although we don't hear much from the Blakes these days," Dobbie said, frowning in concern. The new ranch hands at the Blakes' had everyone in the area upset. Kitty wondered how much worse it would be if everyone knew they were carrying automatic rifles everywhere they went.

"He's really cute," Maggie said.

"He seemed standoffish," Mathew said, and Kitty blinked at him in surprise. It was the first unkind thing she had ever heard him say. Maybe Dante was right. Maybe all Mathew needed was a push in the right direction, and he might notice her, so long as that didn't hurt Maggie. Kitty smiled. Maggie would most likely welcome the opportunity to see her best friend and her sister together; she was that type of girl.

She realized everyone was sitting around staring at her and waiting for her to comment, so she fished for something to say. "Cecily left, and I think he's lonely."

That statement brought more questions than she had answers for. "Why did Cecily leave? Where did she go? How long will she be gone? How long is Dante staying? Why did he come? Are he and his father getting along?"

The questions came faster than she could answer, and they flew at her so rapidly she had no idea who said what. "I don't know," she answered as a blanket statement to all of them.

"But you're going to see him again, right?" This came from Maggie.

Kitty and Mathew both looked at her suspiciously. Was there an overabundance of interest in her question?

"Who knows? He's sort of a mystery." She sat down, and everyone left her alone. She was thankful she had spent so many years cultivating her reputation as an introvert because, for the most part, people left her alone. Of course sometimes she was lonely and wished for company. Like now, only she didn't want her family's intrusion into her private thoughts. She wanted to talk to Cecily. She was good at figuring out emotions where boys were concerned. But she couldn't talk to Cecily because she wasn't here and because one of the people involved was her brother. Cecily was a romantic at heart; she might get the wrong idea and think Kitty had a romantic interest in Dante, but she didn't. She was simply curious about him, and about the mystery at his ranch. Why had he shown up in the midst of the strange happenings there? Why had he sent Cecily away? Why was he being so secretive about everything? Why was he flirting with her? Or was he? No one had ever flirted with her before, to her knowledge. What if his behavior was normal, and she was misreading him? Although, he had kissed her. There wasn't any way to misread that, was there?

She wrinkled her nose. He made it sound like kissing girls was an everyday occurrence for him. Maybe it was his standard greeting. Maybe he complimented every girl he saw by telling her she was gorgeous, cute, had nice eyes, and smelled good. She grimaced. For someone who had no romantic interest in him, she had certainly memorized everything he said as if preparing for a test. She happened to glance around the room and had to fight another grimace.

Dobbie had his arm around Libby and she was nestled in his embrace. On the other couch Mathew had his arm around Maggie, and she was leaning on him in an affectionate, companionable sort of way. Kitty looked to the other half of the love seat beside her and forced herself not to sigh. Which was worse—to be alone, or to have everyone think she preferred it that way? Sure, she liked to read and she was in her own world most of the time. But no one seemed to realize many of the books she read were romances, and most of her daydreams were about being swept off her feet.

"I should get home," Mathew murmured.

"So soon?" Maggie said, and he smiled at the disappointment in her tone.

"It's almost eleven," he said.

"Oh." Maggie's face was a mirror for every emotion she felt, and now she was clearly sad, something Mathew was unable to stand.

"I'll be back first thing tomorrow," he said.

She brightened. "Okay."

"Walk me out," he said, and stood. "Goodnight Libby, Dobbie, Kitty," he looked briefly at each of them as he tugged Maggie behind him and exited the room.

"I should go to bed, too," Dobbie said. "I didn't realize it was this late. You make me lose track of time, woman." He smiled at Libby. "Maybe you can walk me out the other exit." He stood and led her behind him and toward the kitchen.

Kitty turned to the empty seat beside her. "We're alone now. Want to make out?" she whispered, and then giggled at her idiocy. She really shouldn't spend so much time alone; it wasn't good for her mental health.

The next morning she woke with no real desire to get out of bed. She couldn't remember ever feeling this sad and lonely before. For most of her life, she had felt like an outsider in her family for one reason or another, but she had always had Cecily, and that was something no one else in her family had. They were remote and isolated on their ranch, and it wasn't easy to make friends. Kitty was the only one of the family who had ever maintained a best friend outside the family, and it had comforted her to know Cecily was a horse ride away. Maybe she was the oddball here, but she still had a friend. Except now she didn't. Cecily was in Illinois with her mother, and Kitty was alone and lonely.

When she went downstairs, Libby had made her favorite blueberry pancakes. Her sister set a stack in front of her, swept her hair aside, and kissed her cheek.

"You miss Cecily, huh?" Libby asked.

Kitty nodded, but didn't speak because her eyes filled with tears, both from sadness and gratitude. She missed the mother who had died when she was eight, but Libby was as good a substitute as she could hope for. She was only two years older, but Kitty had never felt like they were that close in age. She cooked, cleaned, and did the laundry, but she also provided for Kitty's emotional wellbeing. She had always pampered and petted her and Maggie, and smoothed over any of their hurts or wounds. She was glad Libby was engaged to Dobbie and would stay at the ranch forever. Somehow the house was more like home with Libby there, even if she would be moving to her own house as soon as they were married. Dobbie was putting the finishing touches on it before the wedding, and he wouldn't let Libby inside until it was complete.

She smiled as she watched Libby look at the new house from her window. It was close to the original house, and every day she watched its progress from the kitchen window. A part of her didn't want Libby to move even that far, but it was the selfish part of her, and she knew it. If anyone deserved to be happy, it was Libby. Dobbie had said on more than one occasion that finding privacy at the ranch was nearly impossible. Kitty's cheeks pinked with the understanding of why the newlyweds would need privacy.

Hooves pounded in the yard, and Kitty smoothed a hand over her hair, although she didn't know why. Mathew never noticed her appearance, but every day she still tried to look her best on the off chance that he might suddenly be bowled over by her stunning good looks. She smiled ruefully at her pancakes. As if he would notice when she was in Maggie's proximity. As if anyone would. She comforted herself with the knowledge that she was going to college soon, and she wouldn't have to compete with her lovely little sister. Her smile grew. With her luck, she would end up rooming with a Miss America contestant.

"You look happy."

Kitty froze with her fork in midair and looked up. Dante stood in the doorway smiling broadly. At her.

"Hey, Dante," Libby said cheerfully. "Want some pancakes?"

"Yes, please," he said. He dropped into the chair beside Kitty and leaned forward to kiss her forehead. "Miss me?"

She had no reply, so she simply stared at him.

He chuckled. "You're already speechless in my presence. That's a good sign." He smothered his pancakes in maple syrup and took a bite. "Libby, these are amazing. I hope you're teaching Kitty how to cook. It'll be a handy skill for when she gets married."

Kitty inhaled a blueberry and started to choke.

CHAPTER 5

*D*ante thumped her on the back, but he didn't look concerned. "I was speaking hypothetically," he said casually, and returned to his pancakes when he was sure she could breathe.

"What are you doing here?" she asked. She wiped her eyes and nose with a tissue because they had started to run when she choked.

"We had a date, remember?" He didn't look up from his pancakes.

"No," she said, and shook her head.

Libby was looking between them with interest and a smile on her face. Kitty started to understand Dobbie's meaning about the lack of privacy. She decided to shelve the discussion until they were alone.

Dobbie entered the kitchen. Libby started to rise and fetch him something to eat, but Dobbie pushed her back down.

"Sit, Lib, goodness knows you won't stay that way for long." He leaned over and kissed the top of her head. "I'm heading out to the north pasture, and I won't be home until supper."

"I'll pack you a lunch," she said.

"I have food," he said.

She wrinkled her nose. "Beef jerky is not food."

He chuckled. "Countless generations of cowboys would disagree with you."

"Single cowboys who had no one who loved them enough to take care of them and make sure they were eating properly," she said.

He smiled and took his hands off her shoulders so she could stand. "I can't disagree with that." He sat in her chair, swept his hat off, and laid it aside to watch her work a minute before turning his attention to Dante.

"How's your father, Blake?" Dobbie asked. Most men in the area were in the habit of calling each other by their last names.

"All right, I suppose," Dante said tightly.

Dobbie nodded. "We sure were sorry when he lost his state senate bid."

Dante stared at his plate, not sure how much he wanted to say. "It affected him deeply."

"You tell him he still has friends here," Dobbie said kindly. Libby finished her preparations and came to stand beside him. She rested her arm on his shoulders, and he put his arm around her waist. "I shouldn't have come in here. You make it too hard for me to leave. If I weren't marrying into the family, I think your dad would fire me. He's not getting much work out of me this summer."

Libby put her other arm around him, gave him a tight hug, and a kiss on the cheek. "He's gotten a lifetime of work out of you since you were fourteen. Besides, I wouldn't exactly call twelve hour days six days a week slacking off."

"Sure you would, just not to my face," he said cheerfully. He kissed her lightly and said a polite goodbye to Kitty and Dante before taking his large sack lunch and disappearing.

Libby watched him go with a wistful look and a sigh.

"Three more weeks," Kitty reminded her. "Then you'll be together forever."

"Three more weeks," Libby repeated dreamily, and blushed when she remembered Dante was there. She cleared her throat and jumped to attention. "I have laundry to hang." She picked up an empty basket and headed to the laundry room.

"I'm not sure my dad would hold Dobbie in such high regard if he realized he had gone soft over a girl," Dante said.

Kitty sat up, stiff and defensive.

He rested his hand on her knee. "Relax. I said my dad, not me. I like him better now. They're cute together. It's sort of inspiring, although twenty and twenty-two seem young to get married."

"You know how it is around here. People get married young. What else is there to do?"

He laughed. "You'd be surprised."

What did that mean?

"What about you, do you plan to settle down young and have a passel of kids?"

She smiled. "I don't think I've ever heard anyone say 'passel' in a sentence before."

He smiled. "I've been brushing up on my vocabulary to impress you. Did it work?"

"Some. To answer your question, I have a difficult time ever imagining myself married or having kids."

"Why?"

Answering him would involve telling him all the negative things about herself she didn't like: her shyness with new people, her reserved nature that didn't allow her to be affectionate, or her ability to lose herself in her own world and block everyone else out.

"I'm a career girl, I guess," she said at last.

"And what career would that be?" he asked.

For some reason she couldn't bring herself to tell him. She smiled enigmatically instead. "You have your secrets, I have mine."

"I could always ask my sister. You two are thick as thieves."

She shook her head. "She doesn't know. No one knows."

"Does anyone really know you, Kat?"

She didn't like to think about that question. She had spent so many years hiding from the world she wasn't sure she had ever truly let anyone in completely. "Does anyone really know you, Dante?"

He smiled. "Maybe if we work really hard, we can get to know each other."

"Maybe," she said, although it was doubtful. If eighteen years with

Cecily and her family hadn't worked to make her open up, one summer with him wasn't likely to either.

"What are we going to do today?" he asked.

"Let me get this straight. You show up unannounced and expect me to entertain you," she said.

"That about sums it up." He reached his fork to her plate and ate a stray blueberry she had missed.

She stared at him while he chewed. He was so *different*. Old Dante had been insecure and uncertain in her presence. Despite the fact that he was two years older, he had looked up to her. Now it felt like he was taking over her life, and she wasn't sure she liked it. In fact, she was almost certain she didn't.

"What else have you got to do, Kat, but spend the day with me?" he asked.

"I," she started, and stopped. What did she have to do? "I need to pack for college." There. That was a legitimate excuse to avoid him.

He arched an eyebrow at her. "College is three months away."

"I've never been a procrastinator," she said.

"I'll help you," he declared.

"You can't."

"Why not?"

She frowned as she pictured him sitting in her room, surrounded by her things. She was trying to get away from him, not draw him further into her life.

"And there's Libby's upcoming wedding. We have lots to do around here."

"I'll help with that, too," he said. "I'll help with whatever needs doing." He smiled at her. "Try and think of another excuse to send me away. I dare you."

She picked at the corner of her napkin while she tried to think of something else. When she could think of nothing else, she let out an elongated sigh. "Fine, then, what do you want to do?"

"Let's take a walk. It's been years since I saw your land, and I can't believe how much I miss it."

"What about your land?" she asked. "Haven't you missed it? We can walk there."

"No, we can't," he said, but didn't elaborate. He took her hand when they reached the outdoors, but she shook him off.

"You've changed, Dante."

He smiled widely as if her words pleased him. "Thanks."

"I'm not sure that was a compliment," she said.

"I am," he said. His look turned dark as he stared in the direction of his home, and Kitty suppressed a shudder. She sensed he was hiding something, or maybe more than one thing. She was suddenly curious about him.

"Do you live at home or on campus?" she asked.

"I live at home and commute. It's a long commute, but living in Chicago is expensive."

"You could have gone somewhere cheaper," she said.

"Northwestern is a good school," he said.

"It is," she agreed.

"What do you do for fun?" she asked.

"The usual."

She frowned, something she found herself doing frequently with Dante, she realized. "You're forgetting I've never left home. The usual for me is reading a book and listening to cows moo. What's usual for you?"

He shrugged.

Her frown deepened. "Why is your social life classified?"

"Classified. That's a good description; I'm going to borrow that sometime. What about you, inquisitor? What have you been up to the last six years? Don't tell me you haven't gone out on dates with the way you now look."

Now it was her turn to stay mum not only because she didn't want to answer him, if he wouldn't answer her, but because she didn't want to dispel the illusion he had created. Where did he think she would meet these mysterious boyfriends he assumed she had? They had no contact with anyone but their neighbors and ranch hands. The ranch hands were too old for her, and none of them appealed to her anyway.

"Interesting silence," he commented. "Although I guess you probably don't have a boyfriend right now."

"Why?" Because she wasn't pretty enough? Because she wasn't social enough? What glaring flaw made him guess she didn't have a boyfriend?

"Because you wouldn't have such a massive crush on Mathew Henshaw if you did," he said, and bent to help her up when she tripped over a branch.

CHAPTER 6

*H*er face flamed, and her humiliation had more to do with his carefree proclamation than her ungraceful fall to the ground.

"You're as clumsy as I remember. It's endearing," he said.

She shook her arm out of his grasp. "I'm not as clumsy as I used to be; I wasn't paying attention."

"And I startled you by announcing your crush out loud," he said.

"I never said I have a crush," she whispered furiously. It was much, much more than a crush. Kitty's near-adoration of Mathew had existed for as long as she could remember. He was her idea of perfection in every way. She was sure no one could ever come close to matching him, let alone exceeding him.

"It's a crush if it's one-sided, Kat. You can't have real feelings for someone who doesn't notice you," he said.

"That's an imperious tone."

"I speak from experience," he said, and for a moment, he sounded like the shy little boy he had been. Her heart started to warm toward him until he continued. "You and Mathew are all wrong for each other."

"We are not."

"That sounds like an admission of your feelings for him."

"No, I mean that I..." She trailed off and let out a huffy breath. "I miss Cecily."

"So do I," he said, and his tone sounded sincere.

"Then why did you send her away?"

He shrugged.

"You're going to strain your shoulders from doing that so much. Every time I ask you a question you shrug."

"Does it make me mysterious?" he asked.

"No, it makes you smug and annoying."

"Smug and annoying is a step up from pitiful and pathetic," he said.

"What are you talking about?"

"Nothing," he said. They were deep into the woods now. He stopped and looked around. "Do you know where we are?"

She stopped and looked around in alarm. "Not exactly."

Strangely, this brought a smile. "Lost and alone in the woods. What should we do?" He took a step toward her.

She took a step back. "Figure out which way is south and head home," she said seriously.

"I'll stand back and watch while you astound me with your great knowledge," he said, but his tone sounded genuine.

She racked her brain for a way to tell directions. She knew better than to trust the moss. People once believed moss only grew on the north side of trees, but that had been proven incorrect and unreliable. Finally she took a straight stick and stood it in the ground so no shadow showed. When the sun began to move, a shadow appeared on the ground.

"This is the east," she said, and pointed toward the shadow. "So this way is south." She started to head toward what she hoped was the south. *Knowledge, don't fail me now*, she thought. She heaved a sigh of relief when light filtered through up ahead, and she could see the edge of the forest.

Dante gave a soft wolf whistle in appreciation. "I do like a girl with brains," he said.

"You only date smart girls, then?" she asked, and could have bitten her tongue at the look of amusement he gave her.

"You're curious about the girls I date?"

"No," she lied. "I'm curious about how you're going to dodge the question."

"Like this," he said, then he faced forward and didn't say another word.

She looked around for a rock to throw at the back of his head. New Dante was smug and condescending, she decided. Add that to her growing list of things she didn't like about him, and it was turning into a long list. How did he and Cecily turn out so differently? Well that was a no-brainer. Cecily had been her father's favorite while Dante had received the brunt of his criticism. Her father wasn't the most emotional or communicative man, but Kitty knew he loved her deeply and was proud of her for the person she was.

She couldn't imagine what it must be like not to have a father's love. Not only did he not have his father's love, but he had his censure. She would have to take that into consideration and be more patient with him. Maybe being here dredged up unpleasant memories and made him difficult to like. Come to think of it, he did seem nervous and on edge. She moved closer to study him. There were bags under his eyes, and his bottom lip was chapped as if he had been biting it. She looked at his hands and noticed his nails were down to the quick. She wondered if he was a nail biter.

He stopped abruptly and grasped her upper arms to keep her from bumping into him.

"Why are you staring at me that way?" he asked defensively.

She blinked up at him. He was very close, and he smelled like aftershave. The scent and his closeness were having a befuddling effect on her. She wondered if he felt the same way because his hands on her arms grew gentle and slid around to her back.

"What is it, Kat?" he asked softly.

"I'm trying to figure something out," she murmured.

"What?" He inched closer, and now her gaze rested on his mouth.

"Why you're worried," she whispered. Some instinct made her tip her face up to his, but it was a wasted effort. He dropped his hands and whirled away from her.

"You see too much," he said irritably and kept walking. "Of all the girls in the world, I'm stuck with someone who is infernally observant."

This time she did chuck something at his head, but it was a clump of dirt and harmlessly broke apart in midair. "You're not stuck with me," she said.

He stopped and turned to face her again. "Oh no? That's what you think." He turned and started to walk again.

She wanted to scream in frustration. He was cryptic, and mysterious, and cocky, and, and...Well, she was out of adjectives, but she would think of more soon.

"Are you coming?" He yelled it without slowing down or turning around.

She sprinted to catch up with him and didn't stop after she passed him. She wasn't a runner by nature, but she was angry, and her adrenaline fueled her and made her fast. Behind her, she heard him laugh and pick up his pace so she doubled hers. Never had she wanted to beat someone more, but she didn't. He was well built now and probably athletic while she spent her days reading, painting, or playing the piano. Not only was he about to pass her, but he picked her up and effortlessly carried her to the first fencepost closest to the house.

"I'm hungry for lunch," he said. "Do you think Libby might feed me again?" He set her down and walked past her into the house.

Kitty was left staring after him in silent fury. Of all the...He was so...

Reluctantly she realized she was hungry, too. So she set aside her anger and went into the house behind him.

CHAPTER 7

*H*e showed up every day after that. He arrived first thing in the morning and went home after dark. The rest of the family accepted him seamlessly into their lives in the same way they did for Mathew who kept the same hours with Maggie.

At first Kitty tried to avoid him, but of course that didn't work. If she stayed in her bedroom, he barged right in and sat on her bed. If she read a book, he read, too. Wherever she was, he was there also. For the first few days, she felt an oppressive need to get away from him, and then she became used to him and almost forgot he was there. They settled into a comfortable routine together, and he seemed content to do whatever she was doing, almost like when they were younger and he would follow at her heels. The one difference was his total personality transformation. He may still have followed her around, but he disagreed with her at every turn. And he still wouldn't talk to her about anything personal, even though he probed her for personal information. All in all, they had a decidedly strange relationship. They spent fourteen hours a day together every day, but they knew nothing about each other. She was comfortable with him, but she wouldn't call him a friend. Mostly they spent time near each other, but he hadn't touched her or made any advances on her whatsoever. She would never admit to anyone she was a tiny bit disappointed by that fact.

At first her discomfort with him had been almost overwhelming, but as the days progressed, her fear of him lessened, and she found herself able to relax in his presence completely. Not only that, but they usually sat side by side on the loveseat with their bodies pressed together in close proximity. In the beginning, she had held herself stiffly away from him, but as time went on, she relaxed more and more until now she was hardly aware of him at all. He was like sitting next to a giant throw pillow for all the notice she gave him, and more than once when she crossed her legs, they overlapped into his personal space without his notice.

"What's wrong with you?" he asked near the end of the second week of his visits.

She put down the book she had been trying to read. "Headache." She picked up the book again and looked at him in surprise when he pulled it out of her hands.

"Come here," he said. He crooked his finger at her.

"I am here," she said. They were once again sitting side by side on the loveseat.

He let out a sigh to convey his irritation at her lack of understanding. He placed his hands on her shoulders and laid her down so her head rested in his lap. This was new, and therefore scary to her. She tensed until he started to run his hand lightly over her head. It felt heavenly. She loved to have someone play with her hair. Occasionally Libby or Maggie used to do it, but it had been a long time. She closed her eyes, and her headache began to melt away.

Dante used his free hand to pick up her book. He started to read out loud, and she smiled. He had a nice voice. Soon she felt like she was floating. Her headache was gone, and her muscles felt like jelly. A few minutes later, she was asleep.

She awoke some time later. Her head was still pillowed on his leg, but she had turned to her side and curled into a ball. More unusual than that was the fact that his arm was curved around her waist, and she was clutching his hand in both hers. She blinked at it, wondering how it got there. Voices were talking indistinctly nearby, and she realized with chagrin her family was in the room and witnessing this scene. She closed her eyes again and let go of Dante's hand. Maybe if she pretended to still be asleep, no one would notice her.

Dante smoothed her hair off her face. "I see you," he said only loud enough for her to hear. She wrinkled her nose, opened her eyes, and sat up. Thankfully no one was looking at them so she didn't feel as self conscious as she feared she might.

"What are you so afraid of, Kat?" he asked softly.

She was too sleep-numbed to be anything less than truthful. She rested her head on the back of the couch. "Looking like a fool," she said.

"When is affection ever foolish?" he asked.

When it's one-sided, she thought, but she was awake enough now to hold her tongue, so she simply didn't answer. Throwing herself at a man and not having him return the sentiment was possibly her worst fear in life. She would have to be sure—completely and absolutely certain—that someone loved her before she could ever give her heart away or commit to another human being. Her pride wasn't much, but it was all she had, and she wanted to hang onto it.

"The chances we take are what make life worth living," Dante said. He took her hand and slipped his fingers through hers.

Her heart's pace increased slightly. To him holding hands was nothing, but to her it was a big deal, and she couldn't let him see. "Someone's been studying his horoscope," she said flippantly.

"No, someone already learned that lesson the hard way," he said.

Another cryptic comment. She was beyond trying to figure them out. Maybe he was talking about someone he had dated in his past, or maybe he was talking about someone he knew, or maybe he was talking about a movie he saw, or a book he read. She didn't know him well enough to guess, and the thought bothered her as it wouldn't have before.

"Hypocrite," she said.

His eyebrows arched in surprise. "Excuse me?"

"You heard me," she said softly but angrily. "You want to lecture me about not being afraid, but you don't open up to me any more than I open up to you."

He opened his mouth to reply, but paused. "You're right," he said at last. "We're both guilty of being afraid and pushing each other away." The din of conversation picked up around them. "Let's go somewhere else and talk," he suggested.

"All right," she agreed, and stood to follow him outside. They sat on the porch swing because the rest of the family was inside and most likely to remain there for a while.

He resumed holding her hand and she found the gesture comforting now, rather than frightening as it had once been. Maybe there was something to this affection thing after all. At least he had provided her with the hope that she wasn't altogether unable to be affectionate with someone. Tentatively she rested her head on his shoulder, and when he didn't jerk away in disgust, she leaned more of her weight on him and smiled.

"I want to be friends with you, Kat," he said after a few minutes of silence. "Real friends who share things with each other and are there for each other."

"That sounds nice," she said slowly. She was waiting for a but, and then it came.

"But there are some things I can't tell you," he added.

"Because you don't want to or because you're not allowed?" she asked.

"A little of both," he replied.

"How am I supposed to trust you if you're not being candid with me?"

"I don't know," he said honestly, "but I'll open up to you as much as I'm able."

They sat in silence for a while and he moved the swing with his feet. He put his arm around her and drew her against his chest. "I'll tell you what I want to be when I grow up," he said.

She smiled against his chest, and he continued.

"I want to be an actuary."

"Why do you say it like that, like it's a secret you're ashamed to admit?" she asked.

"Because it's boring."

"It's not boring. It's a complicated job most people couldn't hope to do because they're not smart enough. We're not four anymore. Not everyone can be a firefighter or Spiderman. We have to live in the real world and have real jobs."

"You're sweet," he said. He gave her a squeeze. "Your turn to share something."

She racked her brain for a piece of information safe enough to reveal. "I have a recurring dream I'm back in school, only it's a happy dream and not a nightmare."

He smiled. "You hated to drop out, huh?"

She nodded. "It was unavoidable, though. When my mom died, there was no one to drive us to school every day."

"You told me another secret about yourself once, do you remember?" he asked.

"How could I forget?" she asked. She had a tangible reminder every time he said her name. Shortly before he moved away, she was visiting their house, and Cecily was telling her about the horrible argument she overheard her parents having about Dante.

"Mom said if Dad didn't start being nicer to Dante, she was going to leave and take Dante away," Cecily said. Unknown to her, Dante was standing in the doorway and he heard every word. His face went ashen, and he turned and fled down the hallway.

Cecily's eyes filled with tears.

"I'll talk to him," Kitty said. She left to find Dante. It took her a while because he was in the barn hiding in one of the empty horse stalls.

"You can still get E.coli even when there aren't any visible traces of manure left," she said when she found him.

He quickly wiped his eyes to hide the tracks of his tears. "I'll keep that in mind," he said.

She let herself into the stall and sat delicately across from him.

"You always see me at my worst," he said miserably.

"Not true," she said.

He gave her a look.

"Okay, true, but I don't mind. You've seen me have my share of bad times, too."

"None I can remember," he said. "You're like the perfect girl. You're never sad or upset or hysterical. You're always there, always the same rock-solid Kitty."

"Want to know a secret?" she asked.

He nodded.

"I hate being called Kitty. It's the worst name in the world, but it's what everyone has always called me. Kitty sounds like a dancer from the 1800's. Miss Kitty," she said derisively. "Can't you see it on a billboard in Las Vegas?"

He was laughing too hard to answer for a minute, but then he nodded. "How about your given name, do you like Katherine?"

She nodded. "But it's long and stately. It sounds like a spinster."

"You have a lot of rules. How about Kat?"

Her face lit, and she smiled. "Kat. I like that. It's fun, but still dignified."

"All right then, from now on you'll be Kat to me, and I promise I will never call you Kitty again."

She smiled. "Thanks, Dante. I feel so much better; I can't even remember why I was upset in the first place." She stood and brushed herself off, and his laughter followed her out of the barn.

"Why was it easier for you then? You never seemed uncomfortable around me, and we could talk, really talk, with each other," he said.

She decided to be honest with him at least a little bit. "Back then we were the same. Now we're not."

"That's not true. The reverse is true. We weren't the same then, but now we are," he said.

She sat up and moved away from him. "What are you talking about?"

"What are *you* talking about?" he asked in the same tone.

She didn't want to tell him. When they were kids they had both been awkward outsiders. Now he was a suave college student who had untold numbers of friends and girlfriends while she was still the same geeky outsider. Maybe her looks had improved, but that was all.

They stared at each other as they waited for the other one to speak, and then he laughed. She was surprised when he put his arms around her and pulled her into a tight embrace, but she didn't fight it.

"I guess we'll have to take baby steps until we learn to trust each other," he said.

"Baby steps," she agreed, and she tentatively snaked her arms around his waist, returning his embrace.

CHAPTER 8

The next week was Dobbie and Libby's wedding. Dante was invited not only to the wedding, but also to the rehearsal. Kitty didn't realize he was supposed to be her date until he pointed it out to her.

"What time should I pick you up?" he asked.

"Pick me up?" She pulled herself out of her book with some difficulty.

"Tomorrow. The rehearsal. Your sister's wedding."

She blinked at him in confusion.

"You're not going to make me drive there by myself, are you? People will think we're fighting."

"Why would they think we're fighting?" she asked in confusion.

"Because generally when dates show up separately it means they're in a fight," he said. "My dad already agreed to let me borrow his truck, miracle of miracles, so I can be here whenever you want."

"Um," she said, as her mind scrambled to assimilate the situation. Dante would be her date. The more she thought of the idea, the more she liked it. For once she wouldn't have to be the loner who pretended to like it. She would have a date. "Five," she said, and her smile must have displayed her pleasure because he looked momentarily dazzled.

"Five," he repeated dumbly. They became caught up in each other's gaze for a while, and her heart started to pound in the new, unnatural rhythm it had found since his return.

"Kat," he said nervously, but then the sound of voices interrupted him. Mathew and Maggie stepped into the room hand in hand and Kitty narrowed her eyes on them. They looked different somehow, but she couldn't put her finger on the change between them.

"I should go," Dante said abruptly. He stood and she looked at him in mild confusion. It wasn't even suppertime, and he always stayed until dark.

"All right," she said uncertainly. She wanted to ask him if he was angry with her, but she didn't know how.

"I won't be here until five tomorrow because I have some things to do," he said.

"All right," she repeated. He hesitated for an instant before leaving. Kitty got the sense he was waiting for her to say something, but she didn't know what it was. Finally, he turned and left.

"Did you guys have a fight?" Maggie asked. She sat down on the couch and Mathew sat beside her.

"I don't know," Kitty said. She was still staring at the door where he had been. She replayed their conversation in her head, but still came up lacking an answer. Had she done something to anger him? If so, what?

"I wouldn't worry about it," Mathew said. "Dante's smitten. He won't stay angry."

Kitty turned from the door to look at Mathew. Dante was smitten? With her? But they were friends, and barely even that. The ground they had gained in the last few weeks was limited by their inability to open up to each other. All the time they spent together must be giving her family the wrong impression. She picked up her book again, but her concentration was gone. The seat beside her felt empty and lonely, and she worried she had done something to make Dante angry with her.

*H*er anxiety continued the next day, but her excitement over the evening helped to push it aside. She couldn't believe this day was finally here. Libby and Dobbie were walking around in a state of euphoria, and their happiness was rubbing off on everyone else. Anne and Will were home. Anne was serving as maid of honor, and Will was serving as best man, which everyone found amusing since Dobbie and Anne had dated for four years.

Despite the fact that Maggie was once a tomboy, she had blossomed into a beauty with a sophisticated fashion sense, so she helped Kitty with her hair and makeup. She was wearing a new dress she had ordered online from her favorite store. Her long dark hair fell in heavy waves to the middle of her back, and her green-brown eyes looked coppery against the brown dress she was wearing. She thought she looked pretty, and Maggie told her so as well.

As long as I don't stand next to you, Kitty thought, but it was more a statement of fact than an opinion. Maggie's hair had lightened until it was almost blond, and she was wearing a pale pink dress that made her look sweet and beautiful at the same time. *Like walking cotton candy,* Kitty thought, and smiled over the mental image. She could never hope to be as beautiful, or sweet, or good as Maggie; the sooner she stopped comparing herself to her sister, the better off she would be.

Mathew arrived to pick up Maggie, but Kitty stayed in the bathroom to primp. She had no desire to see the light of love on his face when he caught sight of Maggie. Libby, Dobbie, and her father left, and Kitty was alone in the house.

"I'm not sure that's ever happened before," she said out loud. She felt anxious and tense. She sat on the edge of the couch and crossed her legs, uncrossed them, then crossed them again. The ticking of the grandfather clock seemed overly loud. Somewhere in the house a faucet dripped. The clock read one minute after five, and Kitty's mind went into overdrive.

He's not coming. He decided he doesn't want to be my date. I made him angry last night, and he's standing me up.

"This is crazy," she said out loud, and jumped at the sound of her voice. She gathered her purse and headed for the door. The family had only taken one of the trucks into town. She would take the other one and drive herself.

When she stepped out onto the porch, however, she saw his truck sitting right out front. He opened his door and stepped out, and then they froze looking at each other.

"Hi," she said breathlessly. She had missed him, and the realization squeezed the air from her lungs.

"Hi," he said, and he sounded hesitant.

They each took a step forward and stopped.

"You look amazing," he said. "I've never seen you so dressed up before."

"You look nice, too," she said. He was wearing khaki pants and a dress shirt with the sleeves rolled up a few times.

He looked down self-consciously. "Thanks. I didn't bring many dress clothes."

She clasped her hands behind her back. "Did you have a good day?"

"Yes. Did you?"

"Everyone is very excited," she said. She had been too upset over his abrupt departure and absence to truly have a good day.

"But did *you* have a good day?" he pressed. He took another step closer.

She swallowed hard. Why was it so difficult to say? Why was he making her put herself out here this way? "I've had better," she said.

He looked disappointed, but he was apparently willing to let it go because he held out his hand to her. She came forward, and he helped her into the truck.

They sat in silence as he started to drive. It wasn't a companionable silence like the ones that had developed between them lately. She knew she had to say something. It was her turn. He had put himself out by coming to her house every day, and if she didn't respond in some way, she might hurt him irreparably.

"I missed you," she said softly. "I was sorry you left early last night, and I missed you today." She looked out the window. Her skin flashed from hot to cold and then back to hot again. Had she said too much? Had she given too much of herself away?

He touched her hand. She started and looked at him as he picked up her hand and kissed the back of it. "I missed you, Kat. You've become the best part of my time here."

They shared a brief smile before he turned his attention back to the road. He kept her hand. "Tell me about today," he commanded.

Unconsciously she had been storing away nuggets of information to share with him throughout the day.

"Libby made Dobbie's favorite meal this morning for breakfast, then she broke down into tears, and he picked her up and carried her from the room."

Dante smiled. "Why did she cry?"

"Because she's leaving us," Kitty said.

"But she's moving to a house that's two hundred feet away."

"But she's taken care of me and Maggie for the last ten years since our mom died. It's going to be a hard transition for her."

"And for you, too," he guessed.

Kitty nodded and looked out the window to hide her sudden tears. Dante let go her hand, opened the glove compartment, and fished around for a napkin to give to her.

"Thanks," she said thickly, and dabbed at her eyes. "Did my mascara run?" She looked at him.

He shook his head. "You're beautiful." They shared another smile, and his attention jerked back to the road. "Good thing we're not in Chicago. I don't think I could survive driving in traffic with you."

"You say sweet things, Dante," she said.

His face puckered. "You don't like them?"

"I do, but I'm not always certain you're sincere. You're hard to read."

"That's the pot calling the kettle black. I can't figure you out, Kat. But I can assure you I mean everything I say to you."

"It's what you don't say that concerns me more," she said.

"You were telling me about your day," he said, pointedly changing the subject.

"Dad stayed near the house today, almost like he can't believe the time has come when he's going to have to let one of us go. I don't remember him staying home all day since Mom was sick."

"It must be hard to watch your little girls grow up and get married, even for guys like our dads who pretend they don't have feelings," he said. "I doubt Dad will ever think anyone is good enough for Cecily."

"How is she? Have you talked to her lately?"

He shook his head. "No, she's mad at me. But I did talk to Mom, and she said Cecily is thriving in her new location." They reached the church. He switched off the truck and turned to face her. "And I have a surprise for you."

Her heart started to thrum. "What?"

"Mom wants us to come for Cecily's birthday in a couple of weeks."

"Us?" Kitty repeated.

He pointed between them. "You and me, me and you. It's a surprise, though, you can't tell her."

"I'm going to Chicago?" Kitty asked excitedly. She bobbed up and down on the seat.

Dante smiled. "If I had known it would make you this happy I would have suggested we move there for the summer."

She giggled.

"You giggle? I didn't know you had it in you." He opened his door and came around to lift her down. When he opened her door, Kitty impulsively hugged him around the neck.

She regretted her hasty action when he froze in her embrace.

"Sorry," she whispered weakly and let him go.

"Why?" He pulled away to look at her.

She flushed, embarrassed. She had no idea what she was doing, and there was no book to tell her how to do it. She hated the feeling of bumbling through their strange and confusing relationship.

"I liked that you hugged me," he said softly. He settled his hands on her waist and moved his head down until he caught her eye. "You took me by surprise is all."

"Do you want me to warn you in the future?" she asked, and she was only half joking. Maybe she was supposed to call out a warning, although, saying "I'm going to hug you now," wouldn't make things less awkward.

"Promise me there's going to be a future, and I won't ever need a warning," he said.

She was flustered, so she stared at her hands in her lap and tried to think what to do or say. He used his index finger to tip her face up.

"You're overthinking things, Kat. Let it flow."

"Not my thing, Dante. I deal in hard evidence and concrete facts. Feelings can't be pinned down or proved, and they make me nervous."

"It's not so different for me. I'm a math major, you remember. You're the one who is supposed to be good with words."

"But you've had lots of practice at this sort of thing," she said.

He opened his mouth to speak when the door to the church opened, and Maggie stuck her head out. "There you are. We're getting ready to start, Kitty," she said.

Dante smiled. "I'm beginning to realize why you like your own little world; it's the only place you can get any privacy." He gently lifted her down and followed her inside the church.

CHAPTER 9

The rehearsal went off smoothly and without a hitch. But when Kitty got back in Dante's truck, she realized he wasn't speaking to her.

"What is wrong with you?" she asked, exasperated. How could he be angry at her when the last time they spoke things went so well?

"You didn't tell me you were walking with Mathew," he said. He started the truck and threw it into reverse.

"It didn't seem relevant." Her tone was puzzled. She stared at him as he remained mute and cool on the drive to the restaurant, and slowly, slowly the pieces started to come together in her mind. "Are you jealous of Mathew?" she asked.

"Wow, for someone smart, that took you a long time," he said, and he still sounded angry.

"Oh, I see." She folded her hands in her lap and turned to look out her window.

The town was tiny, and they were already at the restaurant, so he threw the truck into park and turned it off.

"What do you see?" he asked with slightly less irritation.

"That you like Maggie. You're right; I don't know why it took me so long to figure out. I should have seen it from the beginning with all the time you spent at our house and the way you puffed up like a rooster whenever Mathew entered the room. I have to tell you, though, those two are thick as thieves and have been for years. You're going to have a fight on your hands." She would have said more, but he was bent over the steering wheel laughing now. If there was one thing she couldn't stand, it was to be laughed at, so she reached for the door, but he grasped her arm and held her back.

"I'm sorry, it's funny. You're clueless, Kat." He sat up and tried to rein in his amusement. "Have you really never done this before?"

"Done what?" she asked icily.

"This. What we're doing now. Dating."

"We're dating?" she asked.

He snorted a laugh and clapped his hand over his mouth. He cleared his throat. "Sorry. Yes, we're dating. Have you ever dated anyone before?"

Her pride stung, but she had to be truthful. "No."

His amusement fled, and he touched the tip of her hair. "How is that possible?"

She wasn't sure how to answer that, and she was momentarily bewildered by the depth of affection and attraction she read in his eyes. He truly thought she was beautiful, and for a moment she *felt* beautiful. A strange sort of tension hummed between them, and Kitty's heart began to somersault. She leaned toward him slightly, and they heard a "Tap, tap, tap" sound on her window.

"Aren't you hungry?" It was Dobbie, and he was grinning at Kitty. "Payback," he mouthed so only she could see. Then he turned to run up the steps of the restaurant. In spite of herself, she laughed.

"What was that about?" Dante asked.

"I may or may not have interrupted a few such moments like these between him and Libby when they first got together," she said.

"Kat, I wouldn't have guessed you had it in you."

"I didn't do it on purpose," she said defensively. "It was fascinating to watch two people I had known forever fall in love. You should have seen how they were together. I wanted to write some sort of case study on them, but couldn't think where to send it to have it published." She paused. "All right, maybe I did sneak up on them on purpose a few times, but it was funny to see how long it would take them to realize I was in the room."

He took her hand to lead her into the restaurant. Some part of her brain noted she didn't mind at all that her family saw, and she congratulated herself on having reached this level of maturity.

She soon questioned her maturity level when Dante explained the tradition of clinking drinking glasses to her. Whenever anyone touched their silverware to their glass, Libby and Dobbie had to kiss, and Kitty did it so much her father threatened to take her utensils away.

"Payback," she mouthed to Dobbie.

"Remember that word, little sister," he said, and tipped his glass to her and Dante before kissing Libby again.

Her face flushed crimson. Surely Dante wouldn't think she had any marriage designs on him, would he? She would be mortified if he thought she was chasing him with any intent. She chanced a glance at him from under her lashes and relaxed when he looked nonchalant. He seemed not to notice Dobbie's comment at all, and when he caught her stare he smiled at her. She smiled and dropped her eyes, feeling suddenly shy. No one had warned her romance was this complex. She hadn't expected to feel so many conflicting emotions at once, and she hadn't expected everything to feel foreign to her. Wasn't it supposed to be easy? Will and Anne and Libby and Dobbie made it look easy. Was she once again the oddball because she was the only one who found dating complicated?

"A penny for your thoughts," Dante whispered.

His breath blew warm on her ear, and she fought the urge to shiver. "It's going to take much more than that," she said.

"Let's trade," he said. "I'll tell you one of mine, and you can tell me one of yours."

"You first," she said, and he chuckled.

"I was thinking this world is more real than where I live in Chicago. Libby and Dobbie are young, but they're building a life together working off the land. You can tell they'll be together forever and, most likely, happy all of that time. The people where I live don't get married until their thirties, and when they do, they're still as messed up and clueless as they were when they were eighteen. And then most of them end up getting divorced anyway."

"Interesting," she said, and she meant it. She never would have guessed he was thinking something that deep.

"Your turn," he said.

"I was thinking they make it look easy when it's not," she said.

"'The course of true love never did run smooth,'" he quoted, and she smiled at him in surprise.

"Are you a Shakespeare fan?" she asked.

"I would love to say yes because I know you are, but the truth is I studied that play in high school and some quotes stuck in my head."

"*A Midsummer Night's Dream* is one of my favorites," she said.

He took her hand and leaned closer so only she could hear him. "'Love looks not with the eyes, but with the mind, and therefore is winged Cupid painted blind.'" He lifted her hand to his lips and kissed it.

She had always dreamed of finding a man who would lovingly quote poetry and Shakespeare to her, but now that she was confronted with one, she had no idea what to do with him.

"Um," she said dumbly, and blushed while she tried to search her blank mind for a response. Beside her, Maggie clinked her glass, and she was able to turn her gaze to the front of the room to watch Libby and Dobbie kiss.

"Haven't you all seen us kiss enough by now?" Dobbie asked, although there was no rancor in his tone. "We've all practically lived together for most of our lives."

"But the kissing has only been going on a couple of years," Anne volunteered.

"Or so you think," Libby said mischievously, and laughed when Anne threw her dinner roll at her.

"This is weird," Dante commented.

"What?" Kitty asked.

"Them." He used his hand to indicate Libby, Dobbie, Will, and

Anne. "I mean, Dobbie and Anne dated forever and now suddenly he's marrying her sister."

"It's not sudden. Anne hasn't lived at home for four years."

"Even so, it's weird. How did you turn out so normal?" He looked at her in the affectionate way he had in the car, but this time she was too amused to be befuddled.

"Me? Normal? You think I'm the normal one?" He nodded. She had always considered herself to be the unnatural outsider, but now Dante was telling her he thought she was the normal one in the family. She sat up a little straighter. Maybe she was normal. Maybe her insecurities weren't true. After all, he was normal, and so he must be a good judge of what constituted normal.

The rest of supper was a blur for Kitty as she became lost in her private thoughts. More often than not, her gaze flicked to Dante, and she realized he was stealing glances at her, too. When he rested his arm on the back of her chair, she didn't flinch away, but instead repositioned her chair so she was slightly closer to him. He absently toyed with the ends of her hair, and she felt her mind drifting and relaxing as the heavenly sensation took over.

"I don't suppose you're ready to go?" he asked.

She caught sight of the clock on the opposite wall, and her spirits flagged. It was early.

"I thought maybe we could catch a movie before we have to go back, if you're not too tired."

Now she sat up excitedly. Her emotions were taking her on a roller coaster ride, but she was finding it difficult to care. "A movie?"

He nodded. "The theater in town still works, right?"

"Oh. No." She sat back, deflated. Her momentary euphoria had given her temporary amnesia. "It closed down soon after you left. The only theaters are in Billings now." Billings was an hour away by train. They could never make it there and back and still have energy for the wedding tomorrow.

"What else is there to do? I'm having trouble remembering," he said.

She wasn't aware anyone else was listening until Mathew spoke.

"There's the tower." He said it so softly on Dante's other side that Kitty wasn't sure she was supposed to hear.

Dante smiled. "The tower. I forgot all about that." He turned his smile toward Kitty. "Ready?"

"Ready," she said, and now her hand was shaking in his. Unless she was wrong, he was about to take her to the water tower. It was also the town's most notorious makeout point.

CHAPTER 10

I don't think I'm ready for this.

I don't know how to make out with someone.

My feelings for you aren't certain enough to spend quality time at the water tower.

These were the thoughts running through Kitty's head, but she didn't give voice to any of them. Instead she held herself tensely and stiffly on the edge of her seat and responded to Dante's questions with short one word answers.

When the car came to a stop she swallowed hard, took a deep breath, and looked around in stunned surprise.

"We're home," she said.

"Was there someplace else you'd rather be?" he asked. Unless she was mistaken, there was more than a hint of amusement in his tone.

"No." She shouldn't be disappointed, should she? This was what she wanted. He must have taken the long way home because the rest of her family beat them there, even though they had left before anyone else. "Thanks for a nice evening, Dante," she said without really looking at him. Her hand reached to the handle of the door, but he grasped her other arm and held her back.

"Kat, wait." She paused and turned to look at him, hoping her hurt and confusion didn't show on her face. "I wanted to talk to you about something."

"Go ahead," she prompted. Her curiosity won out over her hurt, and she gave him her full attention.

"Earlier, when we were talking about us, you mentioned you've never dated anyone before."

"Yes," she said uncomfortably.

"Does that mean you've never kissed anyone before I kissed you that day in the barn?" He had been staring through the front windshield, but when he finished speaking he turned his focus on her.

Did her life have to be a study in humiliation? Not only had he not wanted to take her to the makeout tower, but now he was forcing her to admit she had never kissed anyone before him. She cleared her throat and tried to think of a way out of the confession. There was none.

"I never kissed anyone before then," she said quietly. Now it was her turn to stare through the windshield.

He was quiet. Too quiet. Was he repulsed by her inexperience? His next words confirmed her fear.

"That was a bad first kiss."

She would not cry. She couldn't help it that she didn't know what she was doing, and he had caught her unprepared. Surely if she had time to study some techniques, she could come up with something better.

"I mean, I pretty much attacked you with a full frontal assault," he continued. "It shouldn't have been like that."

Her brow puckered. Was he blaming himself for the kiss? He opened his door and stepped out of the truck. Instead of closing it and coming around to her side, he grasped her wrist and pulled her so she slid along the seat to his side. He put his hands on her waist and gently lifted her down. When she was firmly planted on the ground he didn't let her go. Instead he closed the truck door and leaned her against it at a gentle angle.

"What do you say we do things properly?" he asked. She couldn't answer even if she knew what to say because her throat was suddenly dry and unable to function. He wasn't discouraged by her lack of reply though. "Kat, can I kiss you?"

Say yes, dummy, she thought, but she couldn't. She nodded instead. He crooked his finger under her chin and lifted it to meet his as his mouth descended softly on hers. His lips were warm, soft, and gentle, and for the first time in her life all rational thought fled. All she knew was that she didn't want it to end. Ever. That's why when he started to pull away, she didn't let him. Instinct took over where knowledge failed. She stretched up onto her toes slightly and wove her fingers into his hair to draw him closer. One of his hands settled on her waist while the other pressed flat against the truck, and the thought he might need support urged her on. Maybe he was as affected as she was. She hoped so, or she was going to look really foolish, but she forgot to care as the kiss deepened again, and he tugged her closer.

The slamming of the screen door jerked them back to the present and out of their kiss. He pulled away slightly and rested his hands on her shoulders so his thumbs smoothed down the sides of her neck.

"Better than the first time?" he whispered.

She nodded.

"You're not going to slug me again, are you?" he asked.

Only if you don't kiss me again, she wanted to say, but they weren't at the point with each other where she could comfortably say quippy things to him, so she smiled and shook her head. There was one thought that wouldn't stay contained, and it erupted from her before she could stop it.

"Why didn't you take me to the tower?" She wanted to slap her hand over her mouth and pretend she hadn't spoken, but it was too late.

"You don't strike me as the water tower type of girl," he said.

She nodded absently because she wasn't sure what he meant by that. Her eyes found a spot on his chest and stared. "Maybe I could be, if I tried."

When he chuckled, his voice sounded husky, and she looked up at him. "Practice makes perfect," he said, and he kissed her again.

After a few more minutes he reluctantly let her go.

"I'll meet you tomorrow at the wedding," he said. She would be riding with her family in order to get there early for pictures. "You'll ride home with me, right?"

Was that uncertainty she heard in his voice? "Of course," she said, and he smiled.

She smiled.

Neither of them seemed to be able to do anything but smile, and neither of them was able to stop.

He touched his fingertips gently to her lips. "Swollen. Sorry."

"Totally worth it," she said, and smiled again at his look of surprise. He stooped to give her one final kiss on the tip of her nose, and then he climbed in his truck and drove away.

She tried to sneak into her room when she entered the house, but Libby and Anne were in the living room, and they called to her. As she entered she pressed her lips together. They did feel swollen and chapped. She wondered if they were red. Would her sisters know what she had been doing with Dante and tease her about it?

But when she entered the room and saw her sisters, she smiled at them because their lips were puffy and red, too.

"Did Will and Dobbie leave?" she asked knowingly.

"A few minutes ago," Anne said. She looked behind Kitty to Maggie who had just entered the room.

Kitty turned to look, too, and then she froze. Maggie's lips also bore telltale signs. "You kissed Mathew," Kitty blurted, and Anne and Libby sat forward interestedly.

Maggie blushed crimson. "How did you know?"

"Your lips are swollen," Kitty said.

Maggie pointed to her. "So are yours."

Kitty pointed over her shoulder to Anne and Libby. "So are theirs."

Libby started to giggle; Maggie joined her, and then Anne, and finally Kitty. When their father walked into the room and asked to know what the ruckus was, none of them dared tell him.

"Trust me, Dad, it's better if you don't know," Anne said. Kitty pulled out her camera. They set the timer and took a picture of the four of them huddled together and pursing their chapped lips. Libby pulled a log of her homemade cookie dough out of the freezer, and the four sisters sat in a circle on the floor talking about boys, life, and Libby's wedding while they ate.

"What's up with you two little sibs?" Anne asked Maggie and Kitty.

"What do you mean?" Kitty asked, although she knew perfectly well what she meant.

"You and Dante for starters. Are you together?"

"I suppose so," Kitty said uncomfortably.

"You suppose so. Don't you know?" Anne asked.

"He says we're dating," Kitty replied.

"If he has to tell you, then maybe you're not," Anne said.

Kitty remained silent. Anne turned her attention to Maggie. "I thought you and Mathew were best friends," she said.

"We are," Maggie answered.

"But you were kissing," Anne pressed.

Kitty turned to look at her and was surprised to see her blushing and staring uncomfortably at her hands. Was Maggie embarrassed, too? Was she also self-conscious about her first foray into the dating world? Somehow the thought that her sister was embarrassed made Kitty feel closer to her.

"Maybe they got caught up in the heat of the moment," she said, and Maggie flashed her a grateful look.

"Is that what happened with you and Dante?" Anne asked.

Her sister was going to make a great prosecutor, Kitty thought. She almost wanted to squirm under her intense scrutiny, and confess to something, anything, to get out of the hot seat.

"Dating is hard," she admitted at last.

"Amen to that," Libby said.

"Hear, hear," Anne agreed. They tapped their milk glasses together in a mock toast.

"But you're both happy and in love," Maggie said. "You're getting married."

Libby put her arm around her and kissed her cheek. "Baby, if you knew how close we came to not being together at all you might have nightmares tonight. Falling in love was the most difficult thing I've ever done."

"Preach it," Anne said. "If Will hadn't had the determination of a terrier we might never have gotten together, either. The man's a saint."

"Hear, hear," Kitty agreed. Libby and Maggie agreed, but when Anne set aside her milk, her gaze focused on Kitty.

"When's the last time we tickled you, Kitty?" she asked.

"Yesterday, I think," Kitty said nervously. She inched her way toward the door, cursing the genetic quirk that made her the only ticklish sister.

Anne shook her head. "I can't even remember the last time, which means it's been too long." Kitty was about to spring away, and Anne sensed it. "Get her," she said to Maggie and Libby. What followed was a free for all as the three sisters pounced and pinned Kitty to the ground and tickled her until she shrieked with laughter. Tears coursed down her face, she gasped for air, and then she heard it.

"Um, I let myself in." The four of them froze and stared up at Dante who stood in the doorway looking amused. "I knocked, but you must not have heard me over all the screaming." He pressed his lips together to stop a laugh. "I forgot what time I'm supposed to be at the church tomorrow, and I decided to drive back and ask in case it's too late to call when I get home."

There was another moment of silence while the girls tried to gather their wits and smooth down their embarrassment. They were still frozen on the floor and piled on top of Kitty who thought her face might never stop blushing.

"The wedding is at two thirty," Libby said. She smoothed a hand over her hair which had somehow maintained its immaculate French twist. "Seating and music start at two, although I don't expect you'll have trouble finding a place to sit."

"All right," Dante said. He appeared to be trying hard not to look at

Kitty, probably because he would lose it and give in to his laughter. "Thank you. You ladies have a good evening." He turned then and sputtered a laugh. He hurried out the door before his gut-wrenching guffaws erupted, but they heard him all the same as his laughter echoed in the yard and down the long driveway.

CHAPTER 11

The day of Libby's wedding dawned clear, bright, and beautiful, but the occupants of the Chapman house were too busy to notice. After their chat session the previous evening, the four girls decided to stay in the living room all night and have a slumber party, although there hadn't been a lot of sleeping. For Kitty, it was the closest she had ever felt to her siblings and the first time she didn't feel like an outsider looking in. As she listened to their stories, she realized they struggled with many of the same fears and insecurities she did, even Maggie who Kitty always viewed as flawless.

Dobbie arrived at the back door bright and early, but Anne sent him away, which almost caused a brawl between the two.

"You can't come in," Anne said as she stood in the doorway with her hands on her hips.

"I'm hungry," Dobbie said. He tried to dodge Anne, but she was too quick for him and blocked the doorway with a menacing glare.

"You aren't allowed to see your bride on the day of the wedding," Anne said.

"Since when are you traditional?" Dobbie yelled.

"Libby's traditional," she reminded him, also in a yell, and that worked to evaporate his anger.

"Fine, but I'm starving," he said, and then grinned. "You could cook breakfast for me."

Will came up behind him and clapped a hand on his shoulder. "None of us wants that." He had to move quickly to dodge Anne's blow. She still hadn't learned to cook, and it was a sore subject between them. "I'll cook," Will continued. "Wait in the bunkhouse, and I'll bring you something." He walked by Dobbie and picked up Anne around the waist. "Come on, Annie, you can be my sous chef."

When they arrived in the kitchen, however, it was Will's turn to argue with Libby.

"You can't cook your own breakfast on the morning of your wedding," he said patiently.

"But I always cook breakfast," she said, and tears were gathering in her eyes. She was emotional by nature, so her tears came as no big surprise.

Will took Libby's wrists in his hands and turned her to look at him. "Libby, this is your special day. Let us pamper you. It's important for us to take care of you."

She sniffed and wiped her nose. "Okay," she said meekly and sat at the table while Will and Anne prepared breakfast.

When Matt Chapman entered the kitchen a little while later and saw Libby sitting at the table and Anne standing at the oven, he paused and turned, not sure if he should flee.

"It's all right," Anne said irritably. "Will cooked; I'm stirring."

Matt nodded, smiled, and sat at the table beside Libby.

"Libby, when you get back from your honeymoon, will you teach me to cook?" Kitty asked.

"Sure," Libby agreed. "What brought on the sudden interest?"

Kitty couldn't explain the sudden urge. Now that the wedding was here, everything seemed real. Libby wasn't hers anymore; she was Dobbie's. She wouldn't be here to wait on them hand and foot and do all the cooking. Plus, Kitty was going to college in a few weeks. She would need to learn to cook for herself at some point. There was no one better than Libby to teach her because Libby was an amazing cook. And, if she were honest, Dante's comment about her learning to cook had stuck in her head. Will might be all right with doing the cooking, but most men wanted a wife who could cook. She grimaced at the thought that she was grooming herself for some man, but it couldn't be helped. She needed to learn to cook; it was a fact of life.

They arrived at the church in two batches so Dobbie could avoid seeing Libby. The men huddled in one room to change into their tuxedos while the girls huddled together in another room. They were giddy with happiness, but an underlying sense of loss permeated the room. Times like these were when they missed their mother most. Kitty only had a few concrete memories of her mother. Most of the others were impressions, or dream-like fantasies, she wasn't sure were real or imaginary. But when the sisters were all gathered together, it wasn't hard to imagine what their mother would say or do because each of them was like her in some way. When they were all together, it was almost like she was still with them sitting silently in a corner and observing.

"Do you think Dad will cry today?" Maggie asked.

"Only when he sees the bill. I'm betting Will is going to."

"No one is going to take that bet," Libby said. "I told Dobbie to carry extra tissues for him." She and Anne laughed together.

Maggie and Libby were the family fashionistas, so Kitty and Anne sat back to watch them get Libby ready. When they were finished, they all stood looking at her in the mirror to admire her.

"You look so beautiful," Kitty said, and she did. Her auburn hair was half up and half down. The creamy white dress suited her coloring better than stark white would have. She looked stately, elegant, and classy, like a calla lily. There wasn't much need for makeup because happiness painted her cheeks with a rosy glow. Even when the blusher veil was drawn over her face, it couldn't hide her radiance.

"You really do," Anne agreed. "Dobbie might faint when he sees you."

If anyone was less likely to cry than their father, it was Dobbie. But to their surprise, when the doors opened and Libby was revealed, Dobbie gasped and his eyes filled with tears. He did nothing to wipe them away or hide them, and the remaining three sisters had a hard time ripping their eyes off him. None of them had ever seen him cry before. Kitty found herself choked up and had to borrow a tissue from Maggie to dab at her eyes.

Their longtime pastor performed a short, sweet, and simple ceremony; then it was over, and Kitty was walking down the aisle. She caught sight of Dante sitting in the pew behind her father and Aunt Marie. He winked at her and smiled when she blushed and dropped her eyes to her bouquet.

He sat in the sanctuary and watched while the photographer took endless amounts of pictures, but finally he stood to approach her.

Kitty felt her heart running away with her, and she worked to calm it by taking deep breaths.

"We have a problem," Dante said seriously as soon as he reached her.

"What?" She searched her mind for what could be wrong.

"You're not supposed to upstage the bride."

She smiled, but inside she wasn't sure what to think of the comment. It didn't sound sincere; it sounded like something from a book. Once again she had the feeling she wasn't seeing the real Dante. Was he toying with her or putting on a show? If so, why? Last night when he kissed her, it had felt real, but today she had the sense he was saying what he thought he was supposed to instead of what he really felt.

"Isn't your father here?" she asked. All of their neighbors had been invited. In fact, almost everyone in the community was invited because it was small; they were close knit, despite the great distance between their houses.

Dante looked away and tried to cover his frown. "No, sorry. He couldn't make it. I'm to send his regrets. He did send a present, though."

"Is everything all right?" She touched his arm, and he jumped slightly.

"Fine, Kat. Everything is fine," he said, but the words didn't touch his eyes, and they remained troubled.

"Dante," she paused, trying to figure out how to proceed. "I don't tell secrets, and I'm always willing to help. I guess what I'm trying to say is that if there's something you need to discuss, you can trust me to keep it quiet."

He clasped the hand that had touched his arm. "I appreciate that, Kat, really. But there's nothing going on. I'm fine. Dad's fine. The ranch is fine. We're all good."

Now she knew he was lying. There was no sincerity in his face or his tone, and his eyes focused on a spot just to her right. She pulled her hand free of his grasp and turned her back to him. "I should see if Libby needs help."

He exhaled loudly, but he didn't speak as she walked away. He was waiting for her in the lobby when she finished helping Libby.

"Ready?" he asked. His tone was polite, but distant. She nodded and followed him to his car. He opened the door and started to help her up, but she hiked up her dress and jumped in. Perhaps it wasn't her most ladylike maneuver, but she didn't want him to touch her right now.

The drive to the reception was short, tense, and silent. He didn't attempt to help her down so she had to hold on to the door of the tall truck and lower herself down without flashing everyone in the parking lot.

Several people stopped them to say hello on the way inside. Any excuse for the people in their community to get together was a celebration, and everyone was in high spirits. Most of them remembered Dante, and those who didn't looked at Kitty with a sly curiosity as if wondering how she pulled a date out of thin air.

"Kitty, who's your friend?" Kitty's heart sank as she stopped next to Miranda Prater. She had only lived in the area a few years but she worked part time at the library where Kitty was a frequent visitor. They had struck up a tentative friendship because they were nearly the same age, and there weren't many girls around who were, but Kitty wasn't overly fond of her. Now she knew why. Miranda disregarded Kitty and practically purred as she stared at Dante.

"This is Dante Blake, our neighbor," Kitty said.

"Really." Miranda drew out the word. "Interesting." She sidled closer to Dante and Kitty felt her anger mount.

"Why?" she asked.

Miranda was jogged out of her trance. She looked at Kitty. "What?"

"Why is it interesting that Dante is our neighbor?" Kitty persisted.

Miranda blinked at her. "Uh, I don't know. Just making conversation."

Kitty opened her mouth to point out that conversations involved two people, not one person saying inane things, but Dante put his hand on her back and led her away. She realized, with some relief, that he hadn't said one word to Miranda, or really even looked at her.

It wasn't until they sat that she realized he was laughing, and she didn't have to be a mind reader to know why.

"I'm not jealous," she said.

"I didn't say you were. All the same, you're very cute."

Her cheeks kindled because this time there was no doubting the sincerity in his tone, or the way he was looking at her.

The rest of her family filed in around them making further conversation impossible. After the meal, music started, and Libby and Dobbie had their first dance together. Kitty watched them with a soft smile and wondered what they were talking about as they gazed lovingly into each other's eyes and whispered softly. Dobbie said something that made Libby blush and smile, and when Libby stood on her toes to whisper something in Dobbie's ear, Kitty could swear he blushed, too.

More people filtered onto the dance floor, but Dante made no move to join them. He sat back and appeared to be content to watch. Maybe it was Kitty's turn to take the first step.

"Do you want to dance?" she asked.

He looked suddenly trapped, and she regretted asking him. "Uh," he hesitated. "Not right now, thanks." His eyes flew to the dance floor to avoid her gaze. She repressed a sigh and turned her attention to the dance floor, too. Maggie and Mathew were dancing and looking at each other in almost the same way Libby and Dobbie were. She wondered what had changed between them recently because now

Maggie and Mathew were most definitely in a romance instead of a friendship. Strangely the thought caused her no pain, and she sat up straighter with the realization. Was she over Mathew? She hoped so. There was nothing more uncomfortable than having a blazing, unrequited crush on someone who didn't know you existed. She peeked at Dante from the corner of her eye, but he was still watching the dance floor. *Great,* she thought. *I've just transferred my feelings from one guy who doesn't know I'm alive to another.*

CHAPTER 12

"Want to dance, Kitty?" her father asked. She wasn't sure if there was pity in his tone, but at this point she didn't care.

"Sure, Dad, thanks." He helped her with her chair and took her hand to lead her onto the dance floor.

"What's going on with you and young Blake?" he asked. Over the years, as first Anne and then Libby paired off, their father had become more comfortable with talking about their romances.

"Nothing really," Kitty said. It was a tough admission that made her sad.

"He's a hard one to figure," Matt Chapman said. "Like his dad. I can't get a read on either one of them right now."

"Me neither," she admitted. "Dad, I'm worried about him. About both of them. Something's not right at their place, and I can't get Dante to tell me what it is."

"Do you think he's involved?" her father asked.

"I can't imagine how. He's only just returned, and you know he and his father don't get along well. Why would he seek out his estranged son, only to involve him in something illegal?"

"What makes you say it's illegal?" he asked, and tightened the pressure of his hold.

"I don't know for sure, but things don't feel right. And they're carrying guns. Not guns like you and our hands carry. I mean they're carrying automatic rifles. They're AK47's, I think."

Her father frowned. "You're right, that doesn't sound good. Keep a sharp eye, and report to me anything else you see or hear, but be careful."

Was her father asking her to spy on Dante? Could she do that? She glanced at him still sitting at the table. He was watching her dance with her father now, and his face was wiped clean of any expression. "All right," she agreed. If Dante was involved in something illegal, she would tell her father, no matter how confusing her feelings for him were at the moment.

"May I cut in?" The polite voice could only belong to one person, and Kitty looked up to see Mathew Henshaw smiling down at her and extending his hand.

"Sure," her father agreed readily. He handed her over and went to talk to some of the other ranchers who were standing near the buffet.

"Where's Maggie?" she asked. She knew he would never be dancing with her if Maggie was available.

"Searching for a bandage. She has a blister on her foot." He smiled and shook his head. "I told that girl she had to start wearing shoes, or her feet would never fit in them again."

Kitty smiled. "You really love her, don't you Mathew?"

"More than my life," he answered seriously.

"I'm glad," she said. She awkwardly patted his shoulder. She had danced with him many times before, but they had never touched beyond that.

"Someday you'll be my sister," he said confidently. "Is it weird we're the same age?"

"It never has been before, so I don't see any reason it will be in the future. Besides, Maggie and I are close in age. It would be weird if you and I were forty and she was still only sixteen."

He grimaced. "Gross, Kitty."

Her smile fled as she caught sight of Dante out of the corner of her eye. Could she ask Mathew what she wanted without dying of embarrassment? "Maybe we could get an advance on the brother thing and you could give me some advice," she said. She knew her cheeks were pink, but there was nothing she could do to stop the blush.

"Fire away," Mathew said.

"I'm not sure I have a specific question, more of a situation. I thought maybe Dante liked me, but today he's acting strange, and I just don't know what to do. Everything is so difficult."

Mathew gave her a sympathetic smile. "I've loved the same girl for as long as I can remember, so maybe I'm not the best person to give you advice. But I'm a guy, and I do have a good idea how other guys operate, so let's give this a try." He leaned close so he could whisper in her ear. "If my theory is correct Dante will be here by the time we finish this conversation. Now you whisper something in my ear."

She stood on her toes to reach him. "What if he's not?"

Mathew stooped low so he was close to her ear again. "Then have fun at college, and don't give the moron another thought."

She giggled, and her eyes widened in shock when Dante tapped Mathew on the shoulder.

"May I cut in?" he asked. To say his tone was cool would be an understatement.

"Sure," Mathew said easily. He winked at Kitty, making sure Dante could see, and strolled off to find Maggie.

It was a slow song so Dante put his arms around her and they swayed gently to the beat.

"I thought you didn't want to dance," she said.

"I don't," he answered abruptly.

"Why?"

He stared at a spot on the far wall, and for a moment she thought he wasn't going to answer, but then he did. "Because I don't know how," he murmured, and now he was the one who blushed.

She had to dig her nails into her palm to stop her smile. She didn't want him to think she was laughing at him, but her relief was palpable. It wasn't that he didn't *want* to dance with her; he didn't know *how* to dance with her.

"But you're dancing now, and we've danced together lots of times over the years," she said.

"That wasn't really dancing; it was standing in one spot and swaying, like this. I mean, even Dobbie and your dad can dance for crying out loud, and they're cowboys."

This time she did smile. "Cowboys have to be good dancers. It's in their codebook, or something. I've never known a cowboy who can't dance."

"Thanks, Kat, this is helping a lot," he said sarcastically.

"As a rule, I've never been attracted to cowboys," she added.

He gave her a tentative smile. She moved her hands from his shoulders to the back of his neck and laced her fingers into his hair.

"I'm not the best dancer, either," she confessed. "This feels nice to me. We don't have to do anything beyond this, if you don't want. I wasn't expecting to be waltzed around the dance floor."

"But it's what you deserve," he said sincerely.

She considered that for a moment. Could that explain part of the mystery that surrounded him? Could he be trying so hard to be what he thought she wanted that he wasn't being himself?

"I don't want anything more than what you already are, Dante."

He smiled and pulled her closer. "I'm supposed to be the one with great lines."

"I don't want lines. I want honesty," she said. She rested her head on his shoulder before she could see the way his expression changed from happiness to sadness, and then to something like anger.

Her father, who was standing back to observe his daughters, happened to be watching Kitty at that moment. He saw the expressions play across Dante's face and frowned harder as he tried to figure it out. Dante caught his look and quickly turned Kitty around so his eyes were looking anywhere but at Matt Chapman.

CHAPTER 13

The days after Libby's wedding fell into the same comfortable pattern as the days before the wedding. Dante showed up first thing in the morning and didn't leave until late at night. He and Kitty sank into their routine of sitting side by side reading, watching television, or watching a movie. Sometimes he kissed her goodnight, but not always. She was confused by him, but he seemed to be under a great deal of stress, so she didn't press him. The fact that he wouldn't tell her what was going on weighed heavily between them, and she found herself withdrawing more into her shell as the fourth of July approached.

"Does everyone still go to the Henshaw's?" he asked a couple of days before the holiday.

"Up until this year. Libby usually prepares a lot of the food, but with her gone, I'm not sure Mrs. Henshaw is up to doing it alone."

He interrupted her. "Isn't Marcus married by now? Why can't his wife help?"

Marcus was Mathew's older brother. "He's dating a girl he met in college, but from what I hear, she can't cook." She looked around to make sure Mathew was nowhere nearby. "Did you know Libby and Marcus used to date, and he proposed to her?"

"No way." He looked properly shocked.

She nodded. "Right before Dobbie came back. It's still a touchy subject between them, and I don't think it's any coincidence Dobbie planned their honeymoon to coincide with July fourth. Last year Marcus asked her to dance, and I thought Dobbie might take a swing at him."

"Why would she choose Dobbie over Marcus? He was like the most popular guy ever, and he's rich," Dante said.

"She didn't love him, she loves Dobbie. The heart wants what it wants," she said defensively.

"That's true," he said. He wound one of her curls around his index finger and looked around to make sure no one was nearby before he leaned over and kissed her. "You were telling me about July fourth," he prompted because she lost her train of thought completely and leaned in for another kiss.

"Oh, right." She sat up and moved away from him. "Your dad already said he's not coming, and without him, there's just our family. So Mrs. Henshaw invited us, but without our ranch hands. Their hands are taking the day off and finding their own amusement, too, so it's just the Henshaws and us." She paused. "You could maybe come as my date, if you wanted to." She scratched at an invisible spot on the couch.

"Are you asking me on a date?" he said.

She looked up at him and wrinkled her nose. "Why do you have to make everything so hard on me? Yes, I am asking you on a date."

He set aside his book and put both arms around her. "It might interest you to know the reason I make your life so hard is because I'm trying to make my life easier."

"Huh?" He had never held her this way before, with both arms wrapped around her so tightly they overlapped each other. She was finding it difficult to think of anything except how nice his aftershave smelled.

"I can't read your mind, Kat, despite what you might think. I don't know what you want, what you're thinking, or what you're feeling. You have to tell me, but since you don't volunteer to do that on your own I have to drag everything out of you. If I don't, then I'm left wondering like a crazy person as I turn your words over and over in my head and dissecting them for any possible meaning."

"You do that too?" she blurted, but she didn't get an answer before he kissed her again.

When the kiss ended, he didn't let her go. He repositioned himself so he was leaning against the couch with his arms around her, and her head was resting on his chest.

"Dante," Kitty said after a few minutes of silence.

"Hmm," he said. He sounded sleepy.

"Is this considered cuddling?"

She could feel his smile pressed against the top of her head.

"I think so."

"I like it. I guess that makes me a cuddler. I wouldn't have guessed."

"I would have," he said. He brushed the hair off her neck, turned on the television, and they watched in sleepy silence until it was time for him to leave.

Their tender affection for each other continued into the next day. Kitty rode with him to the Henshaw's, and they held hands along the way. When they arrived, he lifted her down from his father's tall truck and held her aloft so her feet dangled off the ground. She wrapped her arms around his neck, and they stared at each other nose to nose.

"You look cute," he said.

"You too," she replied, and was amazed by how easy it was to say.

He gave her a quick peck on the lips, and set her down, and together they strolled toward the house.

"It's your turn to tell me something about yourself," he said. Despite their physical closeness lately, they hadn't made much progress in their friendship. She wasn't sure she could trust him, and his unwillingness to open up to her made her reluctant to try.

Once again she racked her brain for something innocuous to say that wouldn't give too much of herself away.

"Let's review," she said as a way to stall. "You've learned my favorite author is Jane Austen, I love chocolate, and I am ticklish."

He smiled. "That one doesn't count because you didn't tell me."

"After the humiliating way you found out, it should count double," she said. The list was paltry. Was that really all he knew about her? "When I was little I had a stuffed koala bear, and at night he still sleeps on the foot of my bed."

"Wiggles."

She put her hand on his arm to stop him. "What?"

"I remember Wiggles. You used to bring him to our house when you stayed over."

"You remember his name?" she asked with some awe.

At first he seemed embarrassed, but when he could tell she was pleased, he relaxed. "You would be surprised how much I remember about you, Kat."

"Like what?" They resumed walking again.

"Lots of little things. Your middle name is Melody. You once ate so many huckleberries you got sick and haven't been able to eat them since. You take pictures and enter them in the fair, but only the impersonal ones you don't care if people see. You cry when you watch 'The Sound of Music,' and sometimes you hum when you brush your teeth."

She stopped walking again, and he did, too, when he realized she wasn't beside him.

She knew he watched her when they were younger and followed her around most of the time she was at their house, but it never occurred to her that he would remember what he saw. Was it because she meant that much to him, or because he remembered everything about everyone? Some people simply had a good memory. Was that the case with Dante? She searched her brain for what she knew about him.

Memories of him flooded her mind, but there was no specific event or conversation that stood out. Mostly she remembered his eyes. They used to watch her and Cecily with a sort of longing borne of being an outsider. She had sympathized with him because she understood the feeling. His eyes were dark brown like bittersweet chocolate and she remembered the tender, limpid way they had looked at her when they played outside together or read books in his living room—the way they shuttered and turned sad whenever his father yelled at him or his parents fought. Occasionally, he would glance at her during those times, hoping she didn't notice what was happening, and she would always pretend to be oblivious. She remembered the way he had unabashedly cried when she hugged him goodbye, despite the fact that he was fourteen and supposed to be ashamed of tears.

"I'll miss you, Kat," he had whispered, and buried his face in her shoulder as she tried awkwardly to comfort him.

Instead of revealing any of her memories to him, she took a step closer and pressed her palm to his cheek as she looked into those same eyes and tried to read them once again. What was in them now? There were new emotions she didn't understand, and some of them frightened her. There was anger, bitterness, and something like fear. But when she touched him, his eyes softened and once again became the gentle eyes of the sweet boy she had known. And then he closed them and turned his head away to break the contact.

"We should go," he said. "I don't want to hold up the meal."

"All right," she said. She tried to keep the hurt and confusion out of her words. Why did he seek out her company and then push her away when she got too close? It had been his idea to reveal something to each other, but when he realized she was seeking deeper answers in his face, he had closed up. What was he afraid of, and why? It was a thought that kept Kitty's mind busy for the rest of the day.

CHAPTER 14

"*L*et's take a walk."

The meal had ended, and fireworks weren't until much later. The rest of the family seemed content to sit around and chat, but Dante was restless so Kitty stood to follow him outside.

For a long time, as they walked, he seemed unaware of her presence, so it was a surprise when he took her hand and laced their fingers together. They walked aimlessly for a while until he sat in the shade of an oak tree and pulled her down to sit beside him.

They sat side by side, their shoulders touching, as they looked out on the cow pasture in front of them.

"Things used to be simple," he commented. He plucked at a blade of grass and shredded it while she watched.

"What's not simple anymore?" she asked. He was hurting, and she had never been able to stand that. Tentatively, she reached out and laid a hand on his back.

"Life," he replied. "There are no easy answers." He threw away the shreds of grass and picked another blade. "When I was little, my life was a nightmare."

I know; I was there, she wanted to say. But she didn't want to interrupt if he was finally about to open up to her.

"My dad made sure of it. He never wasted an opportunity to tell me I wasn't good enough. I'll tell you the truth, Kat; I hated him. Maybe I still do." He looked at her to gauge her reaction, but she didn't have one. It was nothing less than what she suspected. How could he endure so much verbal brutality and not have negative feelings toward his father?

"If you hate him so much, why did you come back?" she asked.

"That's the real question, isn't it? Do you think it's possible to have wrong motives and still be doing the right thing?"

It was a difficult question to answer without knowing the circumstances. She removed her hand from his back and faced forward again before picking up her own blade of grass. "I think it would be difficult to know if the thing you're doing is right in that case. Without proper motivation, how do you know the outcome is correct? Maybe you could give me a hypothetical."

He mulled that over a minute before answering. "If someone was going to harm Mathew Henshaw, and I saved him, I wouldn't be doing it because I cared about him. I would be doing it because you care about him, and I wouldn't want you to be hurt."

At some point she would have to tell him her feelings for Mathew had changed, but now wasn't the time. "Why wouldn't you do it because it was the right thing to do? Why would you have to do it for me?"

"What makes it the right thing to do?" he asked.

"Because he doesn't deserve to be hurt," she said.

"But what if he did? What if he did something bad and deserved to be punished, but I intervened and saved him. Would that make me the bad guy or the good guy?"

She scooted over slightly to rest her back against the tree. "You've lost me, Dante. We're speaking too hypothetically for me to wrap my mind around. All I can tell you is that the Dante I knew would never do anything bad to hurt anyone, and if you're still that person, then I know you're going to do the right thing, whatever it is."

He also shifted his position so he was leaning against the tree beside her. "Do you think I'm a good person, Kat?"

It was another difficult question. If he had asked her six years ago, the answer would have been an unequivocal yes, but she didn't know much about this new Dante. Could he have changed so much in six years? "Yes," she said at last.

He grasped her chin between his thumb and index finger. "I need you to hold on to that belief, for both of us." He said it with more intensity than she had ever heard him use, and then he kissed her in the same fashion.

They stayed at the tree for a while, kissing and talking. She wasn't sure what they talked about, but the subject was much lighter. She felt like he was purposely trying to remain upbeat so she wouldn't probe deeper into their discussion. When the sun set, they returned to the Henshaw's barn to watch the fireworks. They sat close together, and he put his arm around her and rested it on her shoulders. One hand absently played with her hair, and she felt her body relax until she was almost limp.

"Next week is Chicago; are you still excited?" He had to lean close to her ear to be heard over the boom of the fireworks.

She nodded. When she looked at him, her eyes shone with the excitement she felt. "I can't wait to see Cecily, and the city. I've never been to a city that large before." She paused. "Is it scary?"

He shook his head and squeezed her shoulder. "It has a small town feel to it, in a way. It's in the Midwest, after all. It's not so different from here, just larger. And besides, we live in a suburb. We'll have to take the train into the city."

"Just like here," she said. They took the train to Billings because the drive was long. Thinking about his home made her think of something else. "Is there a girl waiting for you back home?" She dropped her eyes and missed the spectacular boom in the sky.

"Kat," he said, and for a moment his voice held some of the intensity it had earlier in the afternoon. He waited for her to look at him before continuing. "There's no one at home." His eyes bore into hers to convince her it was true. She let out a breath she didn't know she'd been holding. Whatever was going on with him, he wasn't seeing anyone else, of that much she was certain.

They said their goodbyes to the Henshaws and he drove her home.

"I had a nice day with you," he said.

"Me, too," she agreed. It had been nice, almost like they were really together, and there was no discomfort or awkwardness between them.

They sat in the comfortable silence of his truck holding hands for what felt like forever. Finally he scooted across the seat and kissed her, and she went inside.

When she woke the next morning, she thought maybe they had turned a corner in their relationship. She reviewed the conversation in her head a few times while she lay in bed; she realized he had almost opened up to her, and she knew part of the stress he was under concerned his father. For a while, she had thought he was suffering confusion over his feelings for her because he seemed to be blowing hot and cold, but she felt more confident now. He was going through something, but it had nothing to do with her, she was certain.

And then he didn't show.

At first she tried to convince herself they hadn't had concrete plans, but the argument didn't stick. He had been over every day of the summer except for the time they argued, but they hadn't argued last night. He had given her a heavenly kiss goodnight. So where was he?

She replayed the previous afternoon's conversation again, and as she did, her anxiety grew. Something bad was happening at his ranch, and his absence made her fear for him grow. Maybe he was hurt, or injured, or in trouble. Who knew what his father was capable of? He had been cruel to him as a child, maybe he was worse now that Dante was an adult. Would he harm his own son? He had already harmed him emotionally; what was to stop him from doing physical damage?

By the time lunch rolled around, she was truly worried. She saddled her horse, stopped at the edge of their property, and tied him to a tree. He was properly watered and fed, and there was lush grass nearby, so she knew he was set for a few hours. She wouldn't be gone that long. She would satisfy herself Dante was all right, and then she would return home.

Stealthily, she crept up the road the same way she had last time. Dante had told the guard to let her pass, but if he was in trouble, the guard would certainly disregard that order—if he had ever planned to follow it in the first place, which she doubted. There was no one around, but she used more care this time because Dante had spotted her on her previous visit. That must mean she was visible from the house, and who knew who was watching?

When she entered the barn where they'd shared their first kiss, she almost expected him to pounce on her again, but he didn't. The two men with guns were still on guard, but they had their backs to her. They were deep in conversation, so deep they weren't paying much attention to what was going on around them. She paused at the exit of the barn, listening, but she could only hear snatches of their conversation.

"Do you think we'll be ready?" one asked.

The other said something lengthy in reply. The only part of it Kitty caught was, "The boss will make sure."

She stared at the backs of their heads a moment longer, wondering what they were talking about, wondering what she should do. What now? She could always go up to the house and ask for Dante. The housekeeper and she were friends, so at least she knew she would get a warm reception there. If Dante's father answered, Kitty would feign innocence. She had known the man for years, certainly he wouldn't hurt her, would he? He had once lovingly told her she was like another daughter to him. He might be annoyed she had sneaked past the guards, but he wouldn't harm her.

She made her way cautiously to the porch and raised her hand to knock when she heard them.

"I'm tired of your excuses, Dante." It was his father, Yancey Blake. "You've been gallivanting across the countryside carrying on a romance like a thirteen year old when there's work to be done here."

"Dad, I told you I'll get it done," Dante said. His tone was angry and belligerent.

"You keep saying that, but I don't see any proof. All I see is you spending every day at the Chapman's with that girl."

That girl, Kitty thought, and felt a stab of pain in her midsection. That girl who is your daughter's best friend, who you have hugged goodbye every time I ever visited. That girl you and your wife used to tuck in at night along with Cecily when we were little. Since when had she become "that girl?"

She was so caught up in her pain it took her a moment to assimilate Dante's answer in her head. "Why do you think I go over there every day? It's all part of it. I need to know what's going on, what others are saying about us," he said. "Trust me."

"I have been," his father said. "Don't make me regret it."

Kitty heard shuffling and knew he was exiting. She bustled for cover and heard the back door bang. She scrambled out of the hedge she had jumped into. She was turning to leave when the front door creaked open. She spun to look. Her eyes locked with Dante's, and they both froze. There was no way to hide the fact that she'd heard everything. His face looked angry, angrier than she had ever seen. He strode forward, put his hands on her shoulders, and shook her slightly.

"What are you doing here, Kat?"

She swallowed down her hurt and tears. There was no way she would tell him she came to check on him because she had been worried about him. When she didn't answer he continued.

"You can't come here, ever, ever, ever. I thought you understood that's why I've been coming to see you every day. I don't want you here."

The only part of the sentence that registered for Kitty was that he didn't want her. She wrenched out of his grasp. "That's fine because I was just leaving." She backed up a step and then another when he advanced on her.

"I can't let you go alone. It's too risky. Come on," he said impatiently. He stalked past her into the barn. She had no choice but to follow. He had been her only certain ally here, and if he wasn't on her side, she didn't feel safe leaving alone.

He opened the truck door on her side and lifted her into the seat.

His hands weren't a gentle caress like usual. For all the notice he paid her she might as well have been a sack of potatoes.

He jumped into his side of the truck and tossed a saddlebag at her. "Duck and cover."

She looked from the blanket to him. Was he serious? By his lack of smile, she assumed he was. So she ducked between the seat and the dash and covered herself with the blanket.

The truck was stopped at the end of the lane.

"Going to see your girlfriend?" The snide voice was one she recognized. It was the same burly guard who had stopped her on her first visit. She wondered if he peered into the truck. Dante didn't reply, and after a moment they were on their way.

"You can get up now," he said, but she didn't. She wanted to stay buried forever. "Kat," he said impatiently. She slowly uncovered herself and sat on the seat, but she didn't look at him. Instead she stared blankly out the window and smoothed her hair which was flying around her face in static-filled wisps.

"Stop," she said quietly.

He stopped. She started to open her door.

"Wait, I'll take you all the way. You can't walk home from here." It was the first softness she heard in his tone all day, but she was beyond caring.

She whirled to face him and he was taken back by the anger in her expression. "I'm not going to walk. I hid my horse in the woods. I may be dense in a lot of ways, but my brain still works for some things." Her voice broke, and she quickly opened the door and jumped out.

"Kat," he called, but she didn't wait. She unwound her horse from the tree, jumped onto his back, and took off, leaving Dante sitting in his truck in a cloud of her dust.

CHAPTER 15

*S*tupid, stupid, stupid.

It had been five days since the disastrous visit to the Blake's ranch, and Kitty couldn't think of any other word to describe herself. Libby and Dobbie returned home, and she threw herself into helping her sister pack up and move to her new house. Anne and Will went home to Pittsburgh. With only Kitty and Maggie in the house, it seemed quiet and lonely, especially because Maggie was always with Mathew.

Alone again, naturally, she thought with no small amount of bitterness. The one highlight in her now dreary existence was the impending visit to Chicago. At first she had thought to cancel, but then Cecily called. She was overflowing with excitement and Kitty didn't have the heart to tell her she wasn't coming. Especially because the reason was her own stupidity.

I fell for your brother and was dumb enough to believe he fell for me. She could imagine how that would go over if she told Cecily the truth. Instead, she shoved aside her feelings and put on a happy face. Cecily wasn't one to look below the surface anyway, and she was completely fooled by Kitty's false cheer. Her only consolation was her certainty that Dante wouldn't go to Chicago. He hadn't contacted her once since he dropped her in the middle of the road five days ago. Surely he wouldn't want to spend the week with her in Chicago when it would be awkward for both of them.

In the intervening five days since she saw him, Kitty had been doing some serious thinking, and she didn't like what she found. She had been a blind fool. Her first attempt at romance had ended in her acting completely out of character for herself. There were signs she ignored that would have caused a blind person to pause. Of course Dante was using her for whatever evil purpose, and she had played into his hands like a lamb being led to slaughter. Well no more. From now on, she was going to be on her guard. Pretty words and sweet kisses wouldn't work to sway her. Her only consolation was that she had learned this lesson early. Make no mistake, it wouldn't happen again.

These were her grim thoughts on the morning of her departure. Maggie and Mathew volunteered to drive her to town. From there she would be taking the train and then flying out from Billings.

Mathew loaded her bags into the back of his truck. Maggie sat with one arm around her and talked cheerfully about Chicago. Dante's absence and Kitty's resulting sadness were obvious, but no one had commented on it. Instead, they had left her alone to stew and brood until today when Maggie seemed bent on cheering her up.

"What is he doing?" Mathew said. He checked his rearview mirror and pulled to the side of the road.

For another car to be on the road at all was strange, but it was almost unheard of that someone would try to pass them on the narrow dirt road. Kitty stifled a sigh and a groan as Dante did just that, parked his truck in front of them, and turned it off. He exited his truck, walked back to them, and rested his hands on Mathew's driver's side.

"I'll take her from here," he said.

"I'm not chattel."

Dante spared her a look before turning his attention back to Mathew. "I have no idea what that means, do you?"

Mathew tried and failed to keep his smile away. He shook his head.

Dante looked at Kitty again. "Come on."

She crossed her arms over her chest and tipped her head defiantly in a motion anyone familiar with their family recognized.

"Uh-oh," Mathew muttered. He knew that look. He had seen all the sisters use it at one time or another.

"It doesn't make sense for them to keep going when I'm already heading there myself. Are you going to make them waste their day and their resources to soothe your ruffled feelings?" Dante asked.

Logic, her old friend and dear companion, had betrayed her in a most egregious way, she thought. She couldn't argue when he presented it like that.

Mathew opened his door. He and Dante moved her bags from Mathew's truck into Dante's.

Kitty hugged Maggie and kissed her cheek. When she started to pull away, Maggie cupped her cheeks with her hands.

"Take care of yourself. Guard your heart. Don't let him hurt you again." She kissed Kitty's forehead and let her go.

Her words were almost Kitty's undoing. She had sunk so low that she was receiving pity and advice from the baby of the family. Maggie was usually the one everyone protected and coddled because she needed it. Kitty's pride stung to be the recipient of pity now, but at the same time she was comforted. Someone somewhere loved her and cared about her wellbeing, at least.

She jumped into Dante's truck without waiting to see if he would assist her. She was done waiting on him; let him do what he liked. She sat stiffly as far away from him as the truck would allow. He didn't try to converse, and she was glad. Or so she told herself. Repeatedly.

The reality of the situation didn't dawn on her until they arrived in town. He hauled her bags out of his truck, and set them on the floor and pulled out two bags of his own.

"What are you doing?" she asked.

He gave her a puzzled look. "Unloading the truck."

"Why?"

His frown deepened. "What do you mean why? I need luggage when I travel. That doesn't seem so unusual."

"Travel?" She looked at his bags. The reasonable part of her mind understood he was going to Chicago with her, but the emotional portion refused to accept it. They were finished. She needed space. He *couldn't* come to Chicago with her. By the look he was giving her, she realized she was coming off like a crazy person. Maybe she was crazy. Her prideful disdain of other girls who acted like, well, *girls*, was now rearing up to slap her in the face. No wonder other girls were emotional basket cases so much of the time. There was most likely some man making them crazy.

Without another word, she grabbed up her bags and boarded the train. Perhaps the worst part of everything was that he was amused by her behavior; she could tell by the way his eyes watched her and crinkled in the corners. She repressed the urge to cover her face with her hands. How could she think she didn't know him well when she so clearly understood every nuance of his expression?

Fate was cruel, she decided as she stared out the train window during the long ride to Billings. First she had liked Mathew who only had eyes for Maggie. Then Dante magically reappeared in her life and pursued her until she realized the unrequited crush she'd had on Mathew was shallow, hopeless, and one-sided. Then after Dante finally, painstakingly broke down the barriers of fear she'd put around her heart, he dumped her. And then she learned it had been a hoax all along. He had been using her for whatever reason. And now when she decided to push him out of her heart and mind and move on, he was going to be her companion for an eight hour flight to Chicago. No wonder he was smiling. She would be like a bug under a microscope. He would get to see the anguish he had caused her close-up.

She crossed her arms over her chest. Not if she could help it, he wouldn't. Pride had been her steady companion before his arrival, and it would have to suffice now. No one had ever guessed the pain her crush on Mathew caused her. No one would ever know how Dante was hurting her. In fact, her number one goal was to conceal their failed relationship from Cecily and her mother. If she could pull it off the way she wanted, Dante would be the last person on earth anyone would ever associate her with.

The gentle movement of the train, along with her plans to thwart Dante, lulled her to sleep. She rested her head against the window with a half smile on her lips. If she could see the way Dante pressed his head into the seat behind him to watch her sleep, her resolve to distance herself might have been shaken.

CHAPTER 16

"Kitty!"

Kitty set down her bag and rushed headlong into Cecily's embrace. She hadn't known her friend and her mother would be meeting them at the airport because she and Dante hadn't spoken one word on the entire eight hour flight and layover. He had said her name once, but when she turned her head to look out the window, he hadn't tried again. Cecily wrapped her in a tight embrace, and then her mother, Shelby, did the same.

"It's good to see you again, honey," Shelby said, and there were tears in her eyes.

"You, too, Shelby," Kitty said sincerely.

"You certainly grew into a beauty," Shelby said.

"I told you," Cecily said. She elbowed her mother. "And she has no idea. She won't listen to me when I tell her she's pretty."

Normally her words would have made Kitty self conscious, but with Dante standing beside her looking grumpy, she was delighted by her friend's pronouncement.

"And she's never had a boyfriend," Cecily continued. "Can you believe it? What a waste. That's all about to change, though." Kitty picked up her bags, and Cecily linked their arms together.

"What does that mean?" Dante asked. He walked behind the three women as they made a line in front of him.

"I have big plans for our little Kitty," Cecily said cryptically.

"What kind of plans?" Dante pressed.

Cecily threw him a look over her shoulder. "You're nosy. Besides, I'm still not talking to you."

"Grow up, Cecily," he said irritably. "You're having the time of your life. Mom told me so."

"That doesn't mean I enjoyed having you kick me out of my house. Who died and made you king of the universe?"

Kitty smiled brightly. She had missed her best friend.

Dante remained silent and sullen behind them.

They took the train to their suburb where the car was waiting in the lot. Cecily chattered happily about all the plans she had for Kitty, but Kitty tuned her out in order to pay attention to the scenery. She had never been in a city this large before. It was beautiful, interesting, and frightening. How does anyone ever find her way around in a place this size, she wondered.

"You can't think of it as a whole," Dante said, as if he guessed what she was thinking. "You have to break it up into neighborhoods. That makes it manageable."

She blinked at him, still unwilling to say anything, and turned to look out the window again.

Their house was in a neighborhood. With anyone else, Kitty would have pretended disinterest, but these people were like a second family to her, so she let her fascination show. "You live in a neighborhood," she said. She had only seen neighborhoods like this on television. All the houses looked the same to her. She wondered how people could tell them apart. To her it seemed like a more upscale version of the government row housing they had passed in the city. Of course she didn't speak that thought out loud. "Do kids trick or treat here?" she asked instead.

"Every year," Shelby said. "There are tons of them. And everyone decorates for Christmas. We put out milk jugs with candles to line the streets, and each neighbor tries to outdo the other with lights and decorations."

Kitty smiled at the mental image. Maybe there was something to be said for neighborhood living, after all. She supposed each place had its merits and drawbacks.

"Do you ever miss Montana?" she asked Shelby. She wished she hadn't when Shelby's face took on a sad, distant look.

"Yes," she said softly.

By now, after watching her sisters fall in love, Kitty knew that look. They may have been divorced and living apart for six years, but Shelby still loved Yancey Blake. Kitty turned her face away. Somehow, right now, a love that deep was painful to contemplate. When she turned, she saw Dante looking at her. His eyes bounced off his mother and back to her. He raised one eyebrow, and she knew he was acknowledging the fact his mother still loved his father. She turned away from him, too.

Cecily gave her the tour, and she deposited her bags in the guest room as they passed. Some part of her brain noted its proximity to Dante's room, and she chastised herself for caring. When they reached his room she stood in the doorway and inhaled. It smelled like his cologne, and it was like a fist to her gut. The room was as impersonal as the guest room, but that wasn't so unusual considering he was living at his father's for the summer. Many of his pictures and personal items might have been moved there. Still, the fact that his room didn't give anything about him away was frustrating to her.

She stifled a yawn as they headed back toward the kitchen where Dante and Shelby were preparing supper.

"Oh, no, you're tired," Cecily said. "I was hoping we could go out tonight."

"Cecily, leave her alone and let her rest," Dante said.

"I'm fine. I would love to go out with you tonight," Kitty said. In truth she was exhausted, but at this point if Dante said the sky was blue, she would swear it was purple.

She helped Cecily set the table and then they sat to eat.

"Everything is delicious, Shelby," Kitty commented.

"Thanks, sweetie, but Dante did a lot of it. Didn't he tell you he could cook?" Shelby peered at her around a bite of chicken.

"No, he didn't tell me much about himself," Kitty said. She met Dante's gaze without blinking, and he was the first to look away.

"But you guys have been hanging out," Cecily said. "What have you been talking about?"

"We haven't been doing a lot of talking," Dante said. He winked at Kitty.

I will not blush; I will not kill him; I will not blush; I will not kill him. She had to repeat the silent chant a few times before she spoke. "You know how it is. We each did our own thing in the same proximity. I read a lot this summer." That was true. She had read- sitting side by side with Dante, holding his hand and resting her head on his shoulder in between kissing sessions. Come to think of it, she didn't remember much of what she had read.

Cecily looked curiously between them. The tension must have been noticeable for Cecily to pick up on it. "Are you friends or not?"

Dante opened his mouth, but Kitty jumped in and beat him to the punch. "Neighbors," she said.

"Neighbors. Okay, weird, Kitty," Cecily said.

"Weird is my middle name," Kitty said.

"No, it's Melody," Dante said.

Shelby started to choke and excused herself to the kitchen to get some water.

"What's on the agenda for tonight, social planner?" Kitty asked Cecily.

"We're going to a club," Cecily said.

"Like a dance club?" Kitty asked.

Cecily nodded.

"Great. I love dancing." Maybe it was malicious to add that last part knowing Dante was sensitive about his lack of dancing skills, but she couldn't seem to help herself.

Cecily grinned. "You're going to love the guys even more. I've met a group of them I've been hanging out with, and I told them about you."

Kitty's fork froze halfway to her mouth. "What did you tell them?"

"That you're a superhot country chick fresh off the farm," Cecily said. Kitty knew her too well to wonder if she was joking. She wasn't.

Dante's fork clattered to his plate as Shelby returned. "Great, Cecily, why don't you pin a sign on her back that says, 'Kidnap and murder me, please.'"

"They're your high school friends," Cecily said. "I should think you would trust them."

"They're not my friends," Dante argued.

"How do you know? I haven't told you who they are."

"Trust me; my friends don't hang out in clubs trolling for girls."

"Well they said they know you and went to high school with you, anyway," Cecily said in the peevish tone she kept on reserve for her brother.

"What are their names?"

She rattled off a laundry list of names.

"Those guys are jerks and partiers," he said.

"But good dancers," Cecily said. She gave Dante a carefree smile and returned to her food.

"Mom, you're not seriously going to let them go clubbing, are you?" Dante asked.

"We're eighteen," Cecily said.

"And, as you pointed out, 'fresh off the farm.'" He used air quotes.

"Maybe Dante could go along with you," Shelby suggested gently.

"Mom," Cecily whined. "That is so totally unfair. You've let me go twice without him."

"Yes, and both times I felt uncomfortable about doing so. Dante wasn't here then, but he is now. He can go and meet your friends, and if he approves of them, you can go alone another time."

With her father she would have argued and most likely won, but her mother wasn't easily swayed, despite her gentle tone. "Fine."

Dante smiled triumphantly, but his intended target wasn't Cecily; it was Kitty.

CHAPTER 17

"You look hot," Cecily said for the fourth time, probably to keep Kitty from bolting away. She was uncomfortable with the look Cecily had given her, but her friend assured her it was how everyone dressed to go clubbing. Her usual sedate look—comfortable clothes, subtle makeup, and natural hair—had been traded in for a skintight halter top, smoky eyes, and teased out hair.

"I feel like a singer in an eighties band," Kitty complained.

Behind them Dante laughed. Cecily had told him to keep his distance, and so far he was complying by walking a couple of feet behind them. He had only complained once.

"I look less like your brother and more like your creepy stalker back here," he said. "Good plan."

Cecily turned to frown at him. "Hush, or I'll ditch you. Wouldn't be the first time, and you know I can."

"Maybe, but Kat won't. She doesn't disobey like some people."

"First time for everything," Kitty said, and flounced her poker-stiff hair at him. After that, he remained quiet and followed sullenly behind them.

"Just like old times," he murmured.

"What was that?" Cecily asked.

"Nothing," he said. He crossed his arms over his chest and kicked at a pebble.

They arrived at the club. It smelled like beer and cigarettes, and Kitty paused in the entryway, unsure if she wanted to enter. Dante stepped close behind her and touched her waist.

"Not too late to change your mind," he said. She eased away from his touch, steeled her spine, and entered the club.

It looked less ominous than it smelled. Most of the people there were around her age, and none of them was falling down drunk or touching anyone grotesquely. Once those fears were laid to rest, she was able to relax. Cecily led her to a group of guys who smiled in recognition and anticipation.

"This is Kitty," Cecily said, and presented her to the group with a flourish.

"Miss Kitty," one of them said. He stepped forward, took her hand, and kissed it.

Behind her, Dante stifled a laugh. Most likely it was because of the "Miss Kitty" moniker he knew she loathed. His laughter was the last straw. Something that had been seething inside her boiled over.

She giggled, and gave the guy a slight curtsy. "Charmed." She batted her lashes. In reality, she had no idea how to flirt and had never had the opportunity to try, but this seemed like something people on television and in books might do, so she went with it. It must have worked because he tucked her hand under his arm and faced the dance floor.

"Let's dance," he said.

She allowed him to lead her to the floor despite the fact that she still didn't know his name. *This is how people end up on the evening news,* she thought. Possible headlines rang in her ears. "Montana Girl Goes Missing First Night in Windy City," being the most likely one.

Her fears eased as she began dancing. It was a fast dance, and there was no opportunity for touching.

"How does a girl from the middle of nowhere learn to dance?" he asked.

"Cows make great partners," she said. He laughed for a long

minute. In reality, she and Maggie had rented a how-to DVD from the library.

"You're funny, Kitty from Montana," he said.

"Not usually."

"Well then Chicago's having a good effect on you. My name's Jaden, by the way."

"Nice to meet you, Jaden By-the-Way."

He grinned at her. "I am definitely moving to Montana when I grow up."

"Better not," she said. "Women are scarce, and we all know how to shoot."

"I like a challenge," he said.

What guy doesn't, she thought bitterly. *Until the challenge is conquered, and then he's free to move on to the next one.* She realized she was sinking into her familiar introvert role, and that was unacceptable when she was supposed to be fun and outgoing tonight. Jaden was watching her curiously.

"Jet lag," she explained her sudden silence.

He nodded.

The song switched to a slow one, and he pulled her into a tight embrace. She was uncomfortable dancing so close to a stranger, but before she could tell him, Dante tapped his shoulder.

"May I cut in?" he asked.

Jaden looked at him in surprise before turning to check Kitty's reaction. She gave a slight shake of her head.

"Sorry, no," Jaden said, but his grin didn't look apologetic.

Dante narrowed his eyes at Kitty and turned to storm off the floor. There were plenty of girls in attendance, and more than one of them was looking his way. Kitty wondered if he would dance with one of them to make her jealous, but he didn't.

As for her, she stayed glued to Jaden's side, and he to hers. They made small talk about random subjects. She had no real interest in him, but he was a pleasant distraction, and he made no secret of the fact that he found her attractive.

After an hour and a half of dancing, she was feeling more comfortable with him, but she still wasn't ready for him to kiss her, which he tried to do as soon as a slow song came on. Once again she prepared herself to tell him to stop, but Dante's voice preempted her.

"All right, that's enough. Back off, Jaden."

Jaden spun to look at him. "What are you, her keeper?"

"Yes, and her boyfriend. Let her go."

"Boyfriend?" Jaden said. He looked between Kitty and Dante.

Kitty pulled out of Jaden's embrace and put her hands on her hips. "Boyfriend?" she echoed. "Since when? That's news to me."

"Really?" He crossed his arms over his chest. "You don't think spending fourteen hours a day every day together earns me that title?"

"I spend that much time with my Kindle, I know more about it, and it doesn't boss me around."

"What's that supposed to mean?" he asked.

"What do you think it means?" She was yelling, but she couldn't stop. All the hurt and anger she had been feeling for days was spilling to the surface. "I heard what you told your dad."

He paled slightly. "What?"

"That you've been using me."

He looked around and noticed they were attracting a crowd. He clamped his hand around her wrist and started to lead her away. "We need to talk."

"Hey," Jaden said. He put his hand on Dante's chest. "She doesn't have to go with you."

"Yes, she does. And if you want to keep that hand you'll move it," Dante said. Kitty had never seen him so forceful with anyone before. It was a reminder of how little she knew him.

Jaden threw her an apologetic look, then removed his hand and stepped back. Dante didn't slow down until they were outside the club, despite the fact that she was running to keep up with his long strides.

She pressed herself flat against the wall. He stood in front of her. Too close, because she could smell his aftershave, and it clouded her thinking once again. She reminded herself to be strong and forced herself to breathe through her mouth.

"What you heard is correct, but not in the way you think," Dante said. His voice was soft. "I have been using you, but in the best possible way. Kat, you're the greatest thing going for me right now. Can't you see how I'm using you to escape the dreariness of my father's ranch?"

"But he said…" She trailed off. He rested his hand on her shoulder and smoothed his thumb up and down her neck. Drat her powerful reaction to his touch. She couldn't conjure what his father had said. Something about doing his job. "But he said you have a job to do."

He smiled. "Of course I do. He wants to teach me all about the ranch. A worthless son is still a son, and he has to pass it on to someone."

"You're not worthless."

"Glad to hear you think so." He moved in for a kiss, but she preempted him.

"You said you're my boyfriend. How is that possible when we haven't spoken in almost a week?"

"Couples fight sometimes," he said. "Doesn't mean they stop being together, or stop caring. You see how it is with my mom and dad. Six years and they're still as in love as they ever were." He took her arms and hooked them around his neck. "I've missed you, Kat. I've been going crazy without you." His hands settled at her waist and he leaned in to nibble her ear.

Her heartbeat quickened, and she felt her resolve weakening. "But," she started.

"Did you miss me?" He interrupted her. His breath blew in her ear as he whispered, and she shivered. "Tell me you didn't, and I won't believe you."

"I did, but…" She spoke in a strangled voice that bore no resemblance to her own.

"That's better," he said. He pulled back slightly to gain access to her lips, and he kissed her with so much feeling she was sure he had been storing it up all week.

"Let's fight more often," she said when the kiss was finished.

He smiled against her lips and kissed her again.

CHAPTER 18

"Well this looks very neighborly." Cecily's voice had the same effect as a bucket of cold water. Kitty and Dante broke apart and stared at her in guilty silence. She rolled her eyes. "Honestly, you two are the most secretive people I have ever met." She turned to go, but she looked more exasperated than unhappy.

Her words caused Kitty to squirm inwardly. There was something niggling in the back of her mind that wouldn't allow her to feel completely comfortable in her reunion with Dante, but she couldn't quite grasp it. He let her go, put his arm around her shoulders, and kissed her temple.

He put his other arm around Cecily and kissed her cheek.

She smiled. "At least this explains why you've been so grumpy since you showed up," she told him, and poked her finger in his ribs. "I was beginning to wonder about you. Tell me all the details."

When neither of them spoke, she tried again.

"Somebody better tell me something or else," she said.

"Or else what?" Dante asked, and there was laughter in his tone.

"Or else I'm going to glue myself to your side for the remainder of your visit, and you won't get a moment alone," Cecily said.

"It all started my first week at the ranch," Dante said hastily.

"I didn't know that was your first week back," Kitty interrupted.

He nodded. "I saw Kitty, and I kissed her."

"You kissed her, just like that, out of the blue?" Cecily said. She narrowed her eyes at Kitty. "That doesn't sound like you, to kiss someone the moment you see him after a six year absence."

"I didn't say I had permission," Dante interjected.

Cecily giggled. "Oh. That makes more sense, and I'm strangely proud of you right now." She patted Dante's side.

"After that, we started hanging out, and things progressed to where we are now," Dante said.

"And where is that?" Cecily asked.

Kitty was curious to hear the answer to this, too.

"Together," Dante said.

"How together?" Cecily pressed.

"I haven't proposed, if that's what you're getting at," Dante said irritably.

"No, I mean, are you going to be together once school starts?" Cecily asked.

Kitty and Dante looked at each other.

"Where are you going to school?" Dante asked.

"You mean you don't know?" Cecily said.

"I told you, we haven't been doing a lot of talking," Dante said.

"I'm going to the University of Nebraska."

"Omaha," he muttered. "That's far from Chicago, but we'll work something out."

He sounded more confident than she felt. Did she want to be tied down to Dante when college started? She liked him a lot, but she still didn't *know* him. Most of their relationship was fueled by her memories of him as a boy and the physical attraction between them now. With distance between them, would he return to being a boy she once knew?

She wondered if he was having the same thoughts because his face puckered into a frown, and his arm tightened on her shoulders.

"This information changes my plans for the week," Cecily said. "A little warning would have been nice. I have dates lined up for Kitty that I'm going to have to cancel." She looked at Kitty. "Unless you'd rather I didn't."

"What do they look like?" Kitty asked. Dante's arm tightened on her neck until he had her in a loose chokehold.

"You're giving me ulcers, Kat," he said.

Cecily smiled. "This is strange, but I can't say it's altogether unpleasant to have you two together."

"It's all about you, Sis," Dante said. "Our first thought was, 'Would it make Cecily's life easier if we got together?' When we realized it would, we decided to go for it."

"I appreciate your consideration," Cecily said. "In the future, I think you would do well to keep me in the forefront of your mind when you make all decisions."

Dante's response was to put her in another headlock.

The next morning Kitty met Dante unexpectedly when they exited their rooms at the same time.

"You wake up pretty," he said as he studied her from across the hall.

"And you wake up delusional. Good to know." She had seen herself in the morning. She knew her hair was sticking up in several different ways, and she most likely had lines in her face from pressing it into the mattress, not to mention she was wearing her glasses.

He smiled. "I haven't seen the glasses in a long time. They bring back memories." He took a couple of steps until they were toe to toe.

It was an odd moment for Kitty because her glasses brought back memories, too; only when she had worn them before, she and Dante were the same height, and he had been pleasantly rotund and nonthreatening. Now he towered over her, and his well-muscled build lacked extra body fat. She caught a whiff of his potent cologne, and the look he was giving her was anything but innocuous.

"It's like you're two different people," she blurted.

"What?" he asked.

"It's like you have a split personality. Sometimes you're the same sweet kid I knew, but sometimes you're all together different."

"Isn't different good?" he asked. He ran a hand over her hair. She guessed he was trying to smooth it down.

"Not necessarily; not if the original was better."

His hand froze. "Better? You don't like me now?"

"I don't know you now."

He pulled her into his embrace. "Let's change that, Kat. I'm tired of tiptoeing around everything when what I want most is to be with you and get to know you, really know you."

"I hate to ruin the moment, Dante, but you're the one who has been the holdout. I don't have secrets. You obviously do."

"Not here. Not this week." His eyes roamed her face. "Please."

She didn't know why he said please, but she longed to reassure him in some way because he looked sad and a little desperate. "All right," she said. She stood on her toes to hold him, and he returned her embrace. They stood tightly hugging in the hallway until Cecily exited her room, and they went to breakfast.

The remainder of the week was idyllic in more ways than one. Kitty had fun in Chicago. Maybe it was because she was with friends, or maybe it was because she was a big city girl at heart and didn't know it. Whatever the reason, she delighted in her surroundings. Cecily hadn't seen much of the city, either, so Dante acted as tour guide and took them to places he knew they would like. For Cecily those equaled shopping areas. For Kitty he chose museums, outdoor art exhibits, and noteworthy architecture. There wasn't much alone time for Dante and Kitty, but she didn't mind. She loved Cecily dearly and had missed her. Plus the three of them together were fun, even if Dante and Cecily did bicker like they had when they were kids. Beneath it was a tender affection for each other, so Kitty found herself smiling at their silly arguments, even when they made her the referee in their disagreements.

At night they usually went out to a movie or club. For someone who had lived the sheltered life of a country girl her whole life, Cecily adapted to the city with alacrity. Kitty, on the other hand, was surprised at her reluctance to visit the hot spots Cecily liked. She enjoyed the places Dante took her during the day, but at night she was content to stay in and watch television, read, or play a game.

"Me, too," Dante confessed when she told him what she was thinking. She had been trying hard to open up to him and let him know what was going on inside her the past few days, and he had been doing the same. She was seeing a new side of him, or maybe she was seeing the old side of him once again. He had been affectionate with her over the summer, so that wasn't new, but now he was relaxed and happy. The contrast made her realize how tense and taciturn he had been in Montana. Now that they were opening up and sharing things with each other she asked him about it.

"It's not easy to live with my dad," he confessed. "Most of the time we stay out of each other's way, but the memories are still there, and they hurt. I spent a lot of years thinking I was deficient in some way because my dad didn't love me. Mom has helped me see that deep down my father is insecure, and he took out his insecurities on me." He paused as if he wasn't sure he wanted to continue, but then he plunged ahead. "You can't imagine what it's like knowing you caused the breakup of two people who still love each other, Kat. I've been saddled with guilt every day of the last six years."

"Dante." They were sitting side by side on the couch. She sat up on her knees to move closer to him and pressed her palms to his cheeks. "It breaks my heart to hear you talk that way. You were a boy, a sweet and innocent boy. You didn't cause your parents' divorce."

"Didn't I?" he asked. There was anguish in his eyes. "If not for me, they would still be together."

"You don't know that," she soothed. "Your mom told you your dad has issues. If he hadn't taken them out on you, he would have found another outlet that probably would have driven your mother away in the same manner. It couldn't have been easy for her to have him dote on Cecily the way he does. No woman likes to be replaced in her husband's affections, even if it's by their own daughter."

She was pleased to see some of the pain leave his eyes. "I never thought of it that way before. I always assumed I was the cause."

She shook her head. "You could never be the cause of someone's undoing."

He smiled. "I'm not sure how I've survived without you these last six years, Kat. You have always known how to cheer me up and make everything better."

She didn't say it, but she was wondering the same thing about him. Before he came back into her life, the world was black and white. Now everything was alive with color and vibrant. The cap was off the bottle of her emotions, and she wondered if she would ever be the same. Gone was the insecure girl who was afraid to hold hands with a boy, or kiss a boy, or even sit next to a boy for fear of making a fool of herself. Now she felt free and alive. Not only that, but she no longer felt like an outsider looking in. She had finally opened her heart to another living person, something everyone else in the world did so easily, and for the first time in her life, she felt *normal*.

"Why are you smiling at me like that?" he asked.

"I'm normal," she said happily.

"Of course you are. You're the most normal girl in the whole world."

She giggled. "Flatterer. Kiss me quick before your sister gets off the phone and comes back."

"I'll kiss you, but it won't be quick," he said, and he pulled her to him making good on his promise.

CHAPTER 19

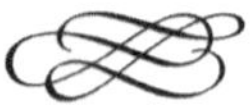

"I've never been away from home so long before," Kitty said. She and Dante sat side by side in their airplane seats holding hands and huddled close together so they could talk.

"Did you get homesick?" he asked. He used his index finger to brush a wisp of hair off her face.

"Some, but I had you and Cecily. I think college is going to be harder than I anticipated in that regard."

"Ugh, college. Don't remind me."

"I thought you like school," she said.

"But I don't like the thought of being away from you," he said. "I'm going to miss you."

"I'm going to miss you, too," she said. Some of the euphoria she had experienced throughout the week was wearing off now. What were they going to do in a few weeks when they had to say goodbye? Would their relationship be over? Did she want it to be?

Dante rested his head against his seat. "I wish we could stay in Chicago forever and hide from everything and everyone."

Her fingers glided over his forearm in a soothing motion. The transformation in him was visible, and she was watching it happen. His smile was slowly being replaced with a frown, and his relaxed posture was turning into a worried slouch. She wasn't yet ready to lose the carefree boy she'd been with for the past week.

"Dante, if it's so awful at your dad's, why don't you go back to Chicago for the rest of the summer?"

He opened his eyes and looked at her. "You want me to go?"

"Of course not, but I don't want to see you stressed out and unhappy, which is what you are when we're in Montana."

"I'm sorry, Kat," he said sincerely. "I never meant to take out any of my bad temper on you when we were there. I guess I have a lot of emotional baggage where my father is concerned." His tone turned angry and bitter.

She resumed her gentle caress of his forearm. She once read that lightly touching that area released stress-relieving hormones from the brain. "I know what your dad did to you. It was horrible, and he had no excuse for it, but if you hold on to your anger, you'll only hurt yourself. I've seen you with your anger, and I've seen you without it, and I have to tell you honestly I like you better without."

He chuckled. "A lot of guys wouldn't appreciate your brutal honesty," he said.

She withdrew her hand from his arm, but he took it back. "I'm not a lot of guys. I like the way you tell me how it is. You keep me in check. I need that in my life, more than you can imagine. Sometimes it's difficult to know the right thing to do, and then do it."

She pressed her palm to his forehead and he leaned into her touch. "I'm here for you."

"That's the only thought that allows me to sleep at night," he said. His tone was sincere, but he opened his eyes and smiled at her to lighten the mood.

When they arrived in their small town, his truck was waiting for them at the station. They were quiet on the long drive back to their ranches.

"I'm probably not going to be as available as I was before Chicago," he said. "Dad has been urging me to do some work, and I can't put him off any longer. I'll try to see you when I can."

She nodded. She was sad, but she understood. If her father had a son, he would be working the ranch from sunup to sundown. She wanted to volunteer to visit him, but after her last attempt to do that, she didn't dare broach the subject.

They were at her house now. He unloaded her bags onto the front porch and took her in his arms.

"I had a great week, Dante," she said.

"I'm glad, Kat. I hope you'll remember it in the future."

"I'm not sure what you mean by that," she said.

He smiled. "Sorry, I didn't mean for it to sound mysterious. You pointed out I'm not as pleasant to be around when we're here. I want you to remember the guy I was in Chicago and understand he's the real me."

She nodded. It was easy to think of him that way when the memories and feelings were fresh in her head, plus Chicago Dante was close to what young Dante had been, only more confident and mature. "All right, as long as you forget dance club me."

He shook his head. "No way. Cecily was right; you did look hot." He kissed her. "Goodnight."

"Goodnight," she said. She stood on the porch to watch him drive away with the sinking feeling something between them was about to change.

The next morning, she didn't have long to ponder her disturbing feeling from the night before. Anne and Will's wedding was one week away, and there was much to do, especially because it was being held on the ranch. The only invites were their family and neighbors, but Will's family was also coming, and Libby was anxious that everything in the house should be perfect.

Since Libby had moved into her own house, that meant the responsibility for overseeing their guests fell to Kitty, the next oldest. For the first time, she felt some of what Libby must have felt all those long years as she took care of their wellbeing. Now Kitty was seeing the house with new eyes, not as a child, but as an adult who was charged with its care and upkeep. In the short time Libby had been gone, it had turned into a mess. Cobwebs hung in corners, and dust bunnies hovered in hallways. She spent the day cleaning everything from top to bottom, and by the end of the day, she was exhausted.

Still, every time she heard hoof beats or a car in the yard, her heart stopped and then beat double time. After Mathew's arrival, she knew the next person to arrive could only be Dante because they didn't get many visitors. She hurried out to meet him and stood waiting on the porch while he descended from his truck.

"Hey, pretty girl," he said cheerfully. He dashed up the steps and swept her up in a tight hug, but not before she had a chance to take in his appearance.

"You look like a cowboy," she said.

"Don't I, though?" He stood back to model his ensemble for her. He was wearing dark jeans, boots, a western shirt, and a white Stetson. Most of the other men in the area dressed the same way, but Dante never had. Even before his move to Chicago, he had preferred to wear t-shirts and sneakers with his baggie jeans. Since his return, he had exchanged the baggie jeans for jogging pants, but the t-shirts and sneakers had been the same.

"Did you have a hard day of ranching?" she asked.

He smiled. "Something like that. What about you; what did you do all day?"

"I cleaned. I am utterly exhausted."

"We're like Dobbie and Libby."

"Except I'm not wearing a dress," she said. Libby wore a dress every day, no matter what the occasion.

"It's not too late. I'll wait here while you change." He made a shooing motion with his hand.

She laughed, hopped on his back, and kissed his cheek. "No way. You're stuck with me as I am."

"Lucky me," he said. He carried her to the barn, and they sat in a pile of fresh hay to talk. He took off his Stetson, and she picked it up.

"Where'd you get this?"

"My dad. Apparently he bought it for me when I was born."

She looked at him to see if he was kidding. He wasn't, and she recognized some deeper emotion behind his words.

"No wonder he's disappointed in me, Kat. He had all these plans for me to be a rancher like him, only I'm not cut out for this life, and we've both known it from the beginning."

"Dante, you're being too hard on yourself. You're not born into a career in this day and age. So what if you're not cut out for ranching? Neither am I. It doesn't make me less of a daughter, and it doesn't make you less of a son. You're brilliant at math, and wonderful at everything else. If your dad can't accept you for who you are, then that's his problem."

He lay back on the hay and gave her a lazy smile. "Maybe you should tell him all this. It sounds right when you say it, not so much when I try to tell him."

She sat up straighter and balled her hands into fists. "Let me. I would love to tell him a thing or two where you're concerned."

He chuckled. "I adore this side of you, Kat." He took her hand and kissed her palm.

"I guess I have an overdeveloped sense of protectiveness and justice."

"You're perfect," he said sincerely.

They shared a moment, looking into each other's eyes, before she spoke again.

"Anne and Will are getting married next week. Can you be my date?"

He froze. "Which day next week?"

"Friday."

He relaxed and picked up a piece of hay. "I think so. Dad wants me to help him with something, but that's not until Saturday. He probably won't be happy with my absence, but I also think he probably won't want to besmirch our family name by not being represented at the wedding."

"He's been absent from all the community events lately." Her palm rested on his chest. "Is he all right? I know losing the senate race was a blow, but I thought he would have recovered by now."

He picked up her hand from his chest and kissed it again. She got the sense he was trying to choose his words carefully. "I think he had good intentions when he ran for the state senate. He's been frustrated about the way the government has been running lately, and he had talked to a lot of people who felt the same. But I don't think he took into account how difficult it would be to unseat an incumbent." He bit his lip worriedly. "He's not himself right now, Kat. I've tried talking to him until I'm blue in the face, but he won't be dissuaded."

"Dissuaded from what?" she asked.

"His political ideology. There are other forces fanning the flames of his discontent."

She nodded. She didn't have to be told the strange men on his ranch were the ones doing the fanning.

"Dante, you don't think he would do anything desperate would he?" Now it was her turn to sound worried.

"What's your definition of desperate?" he asked. He brushed the hay off his chest, sat up, and smiled at her. She knew she was supposed to take his words as teasing, but something in his eyes made her heartbeat quicken. She recognized that look because she'd felt it many times before. Dante was afraid.

They fell into the same routine every day until the wedding. Kitty's days became busier as Will's family's arrival grew imminent, and Dante seemed to become more exhausted and frazzled as well.

Kitty spent almost every day cleaning and learning to cook with Libby. Libby would be doing all of the cooking for the wedding as well as for Will's family's visit, but she couldn't do it alone, so Maggie and Kitty set themselves up as her helpers. Mathew sat in the background and did whatever needed doing: peeling potatoes, snapping beans, or simply opening jars with stubborn lids. Occasionally Dobbie popped his head in to see if they needed help, and Libby always put him to work. Outwardly he complained, but Kitty wondered if he secretly enjoyed the chance to do something different than his everyday manual labor. Of course, he might enjoy spending time with Libby. They were even more in love since their marriage, and practically inseparable now. On the days he didn't help in the kitchen, he arrived for supper looking grimy and exhausted, but happy to see Libby again.

"Hello, little wife," had become his standard greeting to her, and then he would pick her up and kiss her.

Kitty watched the tender exchange with a wistful smile. She wanted to be like them when she was married. Her smile grew because she now realized she thought of her future marriage as a certainty, whereas before she had thought herself incapable of romance. She owed Dante a debt of gratitude for that change, and when she saw him next, she would begin to repay it. Her smile widened again until it threatened to crack, so she pushed thoughts of love from her mind and concentrated on learning to make biscuits.

Will's parents and brothers finally arrived. His father was the president of a college in Pittsburgh. He reminded Kitty of the politicians she had seen on television. He was tall, stately, handsome, and well spoken. He complimented everything and everyone with seeming sincerity, but Kitty wondered if he had become so used to glad-handing people that it was second nature to him now. Will's mother was sweet and quiet, but Will had told them that was a façade. Underneath it all, she had a wicked sense of humor, at least according to her son who had been on the receiving end of a few of her practical jokes. His two older brothers possessed their mother's sense of humor because their eyes sparkled with repressed humor and mischief. Kitty thought they were probably plotting some prank to pull at the wedding. Their comical bouts with Anne were legendary as they tried to one-up each other in the practical jokes they pulled on their future sister-in-law.

Kitty's favorite story was about the first time Will's brothers met Anne. She stayed at his parents' house, and his oldest brother stole her underwear and hid it all over the house. Anne, who was formidable in her own right, didn't say a word. The brothers mistakenly thought it was because she was shy, but they learned their lesson the hard way. The oldest brother had a date the night after he stole Anne's underwear. It was his first date with a girl he had been pursuing for some time. After the meal, when he took out his wallet to pay he found that Anne had replaced all of his money and credit cards with a picture of her smiling face. On top of that, she had somehow stolen his cell phone and replaced it with a television remote control of the same size.

From that moment on, war was declared, and it had become a free-for-all that had lasted the past four years as Anne and Will's brothers tried to outdo each other in their pranks. Will was so relieved his brothers had stopped picking on him that he didn't care they were now picking on his fiancée.

"She's man enough to take it; I'm not," he had said on more than one occasion.

As for Kitty, she was strangely proud of her rotten and spirited sister.

Dante arrived after Will's family, and she met him on the porch.

"I forgot today was the day," he said. "Should I go?"

She stood on the step above him and rested her arms on his shoulders. "Don't be silly, why would you go?"

"I don't want to intrude," he said.

"You're not intruding, and if you go you won't be able to taste the biscuits I made," she said.

"You cooked?"

"Technically I baked."

"Now I have to stay," he said. "Plus, I missed you like crazy today and I don't want to go home."

"Are things bad today?"

"And every other day," he said wearily.

"My poor Dante," she said. She pulled him into a hug.

He buried his face in her neck. "You're the best country girl a cowpoke could hope for."

She smiled and pulled away. "Come and eat." She took his hand to lead him inside.

They had a pleasant dinner with Will's family. Will had lived with them for a summer, and he and Anne had been together for four years. But that wasn't the only reason he felt like family. He was loving, outgoing, and soft-hearted. He had originally been Kitty's tutor, and in some ways she still thought of him as a mentor. She told all this to Dante as they took a walk in the woods. The sun was starting its descent, and she gazed at it thoughtfully. The days were getting shorter. Usually she welcomed the arrival of fall, but this year it meant saying goodbye to her family and to Dante.

"What's that?" Dante asked.

Kitty turned to look in the direction he was pointing. She saw a crudely constructed lean-to. "I don't know."

He tugged her hand to lead her closer. "Look." He ran his fingers over initials that had been carved into the side of one of the makeshift walls.

"Anne and Will, Dobbie and Libby, and Mathew and Maggie," she said as she traced her finger over the initials.

"Looks like we're the only ones who are missing," Dante said. "Let's change that." He pulled a pocket knife out of his pants and painstakingly carved their initials among all the others.

"There," he said when he was finished. "Now it's official."

"Something is missing," she said. He looked at her in bewilderment. She stood on her toes to give him a lingering kiss. "Now it's official," she said.

He smiled. "I like the way you think, Kat."

They walked arm in arm back to the house and sat on the front porch swing.

"I don't think I'll be able to visit tomorrow," Dante said.

"Oh," she said. She wasn't sure she succeeded in concealing her disappointment.

"I'm sorry," Dante said. He caught her hand, and she rested her head on his shoulder. "I want to come, but things are busy right now."

"I understand," she said.

He used his feet to push them gently on the swing.

"Kat, I have to ask you something, and I need you to be completely honest with me, even if I won't like the answer."

"All right," she said. What could he possibly ask?

"Do you trust me?"

She winced. It was the one question he could have asked with the potential to hurt him. For a long moment she was silent as she thought through her answer.

"Yes," she said at last. There were still unresolved issues between them. He was hiding something from her, but after so much time spent together this summer she trusted the motivation that made him remain hidden.

He let out a breath and she realized he had been holding it while he waited for her answer. "I can't tell you how much it means to me to hear you say that." He let go her hand and put his arm around her to draw her close against his chest. She rested her head on his chest and he laid his head on hers. "I want you to remember that in the next few days."

The pace of her heartbeat doubled. "Why? What do you mean?"

He smoothed his hand down her hair. "Nothing. I want you to know that no matter what might happen in the next couple of weeks, things aren't always as they seem. You can trust me. I would never purposely hurt you."

"I don't understand."

"I know, Kat. You will soon. Let's enjoy this moment." He put his other arm around her. She slipped her arms around his waist, and they held onto each other as tightly as they could until it was time for him to go home.

CHAPTER 21

The four sisters repeated their slumber party the night before the wedding, but they stayed up talking in Libby's living room so they wouldn't bother Will's family. Instead they bothered Dobbie.

He stumbled downstairs at around three o'clock in the morning with tousled hair and a grumpy expression.

"I had no idea you girls were so loud," he said. "How does your dad ever sleep?"

"Why do you think he's surly all the time?" Kitty asked.

He squinted at her and tried to focus on Libby. "Wife, are you coming to bed?"

She stood to follow him, but her sisters chorused for her to stay.

"Sorry, girls, but he's much more fun to sleep next to than you." She ended on a giggle because Dobbie swept her into his arms and jogged up the stairs with her.

The morning of the wedding was overcast and cool, but the weatherman predicted a sunny afternoon, so everyone was hopeful things would clear up.

Kitty was busy, busier than she had ever been, as she helped Libby with the final preparations. The only people invited were their immediate family along with Will's family, all the ranch hands, the Blakes, the Henshaws, and some of the Henshaws' cowhands who had been around forever and were also like family. She was thankful for the work, though, because it kept her mind off Dante and their last disturbing conversation from two nights before.

The men were busy setting up chairs and tables in the barn. Will's brothers so far hadn't pulled one prank, but Kitty wondered if they were biding their time. The two of them, along with Dobbie, were serving as groomsmen; Libby, Kitty, and Maggie were bridesmaids. Despite the rural setting, they hired a DJ for the event, rented tables with elegant cloths, and hired a florist to decorate.

Kitty sneaked into the barn before the ceremony and was amazed at the transformation. The barn, where the wedding was being held, was by far their most picturesque. It was built by her great grandfather at the turn of the last century, so it was solid wood with interesting architectural details. The outside was painted a creamy white color, and the trim was forest green. The family now used it as a horse barn, but the horses had been moved to another location a few weeks ago so Dobbie could wash the barn and let it air out. With the beautifully decorated tables, endless strings of tiny white lights, candles, and flowers everywhere, it was transformed into something from a dream.

Anne was resplendent in their mother's dress. It was simple, yet elegant. She wore her hair down with a wreath of flowers woven into her crown. Her bouquet was made up of wildflowers. The other sisters wore dresses of pale lavender. They also carried wildflowers and wore wreaths on their heads. Anne would have had them go barefoot, but Libby put her foot down.

"We're going to be walking where thousands of horses once trod. I'm not going barefoot, and neither are the girls," she said.

"Fine, but at least wear sandals. You'll look ridiculous wearing your normal three inch heels."

Libby hadn't contested the sandals. Kitty was glad because her feet were comfortable, and the sandals were good for dancing, too. She hoped Dante wouldn't balk too much about dancing. He had danced with her a lot at the clubs in Chicago. After their last conversation and his absence yesterday, she was afraid he might not show up, let alone dance.

But when she walked down the makeshift aisle in the barn, he was sitting behind her father. He smiled and then smiled wider when she winked at him.

Anne remained dry-eyed through the service, but Will didn't. He didn't sob, but he choked up a couple of times until it was time for the ring. He turned to his brother who turned to the next brother who turned to Dobbie. Dobbie pulled out a box of Cracker Jack, fished around inside for the ring, and then handed the ring back up the line to Will.

"You're supposed to be the sensible one," Anne said to Dobbie. He shrugged with mock innocence, and everyone laughed.

During the reception, the brothers held up signs every time Anne and Will kissed. Sometimes they rated the kiss on a scale of one to ten, and sometimes they commented the kiss was "Too boring," or "Too dry."

"Keep in mind your day is coming," Anne said, but they laughed unconcernedly.

"Can we take a quick walk?" Dante whispered in Kitty's ear. He held out his hand for her and led her outside. She thought maybe he wanted to talk about something, but when they reached the outdoors he pulled out his phone and snapped a picture of her.

"You still carry your phone here?" she asked. Cell phones would only work on the Henshaws' property because they had the only tower for more than a hundred miles.

"Old habits die hard. Besides, it came in handy today." He started to put it away, but she reached for it.

"May I see it?" He handed it over, and she inspected it. "I've never seen one up close before. Weird, huh?"

He shook his head. "Not to me, but then I know where you're coming from. You might not want to mention it to people when you get to college. They'll think you're Amish." He took her hand, and they strolled the property. Back inside the barn, music started.

"Did you bring me out here so you won't have to dance with me?" she asked.

In answer he turned toward her and took her in his arms. "Maybe I brought you out here so we could have the dance floor to ourselves." They started to dance a slow, gentle rhythm.

"Did you?" she asked.

"No, but that sounded romantic. I wanted to steal a private moment with you and take your picture. You look beautiful, Kat." He brushed the back of his hand on her cheek and leaned in to kiss her.

"Thank you, Dante. You look very handsome," she said as soon as the kiss was finished.

They stayed outside dancing under the shade of a tree until she worried their absence might become conspicuous. When they returned to the barn they danced again. Kitty never wanted the evening to end.

"I wish we could stay like this forever," she said.

"Me too. You have no idea how much."

It was time for Anne and Will to leave for their honeymoon. They said goodbyes, and this time Anne did cry as she hugged her father and each of her sisters. But then Will's brothers slipped on dark sunglasses and pretended to speak into lapel microphones as they herded the couple to the car, and she ended up laughing as she stuck her head out the window and waved.

After Anne's departure Kitty felt a strange mix of emotions: sadness another sister was no longer hers alone, happiness for the addition of Will to their family, and a wistful, romantic feeling for her own life.

She linked her arm through Dante's as they watched Anne and Will drive away.

"Dante, I've been thinking."

"Me too," he said as they talked they headed back to the tree where they had danced earlier. They stopped when they reached it, and he settled his hands on her waist.

"Kat," he began, but she interrupted him. She was nervous about the speech she had prepared, and she was afraid if she let him talk her boldness would flee.

"I've been thinking about college. I want us to stay together and give it a go. I don't know how it's going to work being apart, but I think we can do it. We'll still have our breaks, and we can work in a couple of visits. You only have a couple of years left before you graduate. Maybe you could become an actuary in Omaha." She smiled and pressed her palm to his chest.

He took a deep breath. "I wish you hadn't said that, Kat. It makes what I'm about to say that much harder." He paused and licked his lips. "I think we should break up."

Her mouth fell open in shock. He hurried on before she could speak, but there was no danger of that. She had no words.

"It's been a great summer, but what future do we have living so far apart?"

Her mouth remained slightly open as she stared at him.

"I'm sorry," he said. "I have to go." He turned and fled before she could muster a word or thought.

CHAPTER 22

"I don't understand. Things were going well."

Kitty nodded and then remembered Cecily couldn't see her on the other end of the telephone line. "I know." They had been over it all before, a couple of times, but still hadn't found any solutions to Dante's abrupt breakup. After crying for a few hours, Kitty called Cecily and poured out her heart to her friend. It was the first time Kitty had ever shared emotional distress with Cecily, and she was unprepared for her friend's level of empathy. When she finished her story, Cecily broke down and cried, something Kitty hadn't expected but appreciated anyway.

"He came to Anne's wedding, took your picture, and then broke up with you?" Cecily said. Kitty knew she was trying to clarify the confusing events in her mind, but it was still painful to hear the recap of events.

"Yes."

"That doesn't make any sense," Cecily said.

"I know," Kitty agreed. "But something has been going on with him since he returned here."

"I wish I could tell you what it is, but I'm beginning to realize how little I know my brother. We haven't lived together for six years, and I'm not sure he's the same boy I knew when our parents split up."

Kitty wasn't sure either. "I think something is going on at the ranch," she said.

"I think so, too. I noticed little things were different before I left."

"What can you tell me about what's going on?"

"Not much," Cecily said. "Dad kept me out of everything, and Dante followed in his footsteps. He sent me away almost as soon as he arrived."

"Without telling you anything? What does he say when he calls?" Kitty asked.

"He talks about you. Incessantly. That's why his sudden breakup is such a shock to me. From all accounts, he's head over heels about you, Kitty."

"Do you think it's something illegal?" Kitty asked the question that had been weighing on her mind, but instantly regretted it.

"No," Cecily said coolly. She and her father were close. She would never believe he was involved in anything truly bad.

"Maybe the stress of being back with your dad is getting to him," Kitty suggested. "You know their relationship has always been difficult." She wondered how Cecily justified the way her father treated Dante. Maybe she didn't. Maybe she didn't allow herself to see what went on.

"But they were getting along well before I left, and Dante told Mom they were getting along the best they ever have," Cecily said.

That didn't sync with what Dante had told her. From his account, he and his father were barely able to tolerate each other. Obviously, he was lying to either her or his sister, but which one? And why? Why would he need to lie to either of them?

"Cecily, can you think of anything your dad or Dante might have said or done that could be relevant to what's going on?"

"No," Cecily said. "I'm sorry, Kitty, I wish I could help, but I don't remember anything out of the ordinary. Although Mom has been trying to make me believe nothing about my life at the ranch is ordinary." Her tone held some bitterness. She and her mother weren't mortal enemies, but they did butt heads on occasion. Kitty loved her friend dearly, but she had to admit Cecily was biased in her father's favor, and no wonder. It would be difficult not to favor the parent who lavished constant love and attention.

"Tell me about what's been going on there," Kitty said. Talking about her problems was depressing, and it wasn't getting her anywhere.

"I've been going out with a few guys and hitting the clubs," Cecily said, but there was something in her tone Kitty recognized.

"Are you homesick?"

There was a pause. "Yes," Cecily admitted. "I feel stupid for admitting it."

"Why?"

"Because I'm supposed to be this independent, fun girl. I should adore the city and want to live here forever, but I miss my dad, my horse, and the wide open spaces. I didn't realize I was claustrophobic until I moved to a place where the houses are so close together and all look the same."

Kitty smiled. She was surprised by Cecily's admission. For years she had been dreaming of getting out of Montana and heading to the big city. "When can you come home?"

"Dante says I can return in two weeks." She sounded irritable, probably because she resented Dante's control over her life and schedule.

Kitty fought her own irritation. He hadn't said a word to her about Cecily's return. "Are you going to come home then?"

Cecily expelled a long breath. "I don't know. You and Dante will both be gone, and I'll be lonely without you. But staying here doesn't appeal to me, either. I have no idea what to do with my life; it's a horrible feeling."

"You could stay there, get a degree, and then return to Montana," Kitty suggested.

"You're persistent," Cecily said.

For years she had been urging Cecily to go to college, and Cecily always refused. Kitty had a hard time imagining anyone who didn't want to go to college, while Cecily had a hard time imagining anyone who did.

"Listen, Kitty," Cecily said. "Be careful with Dante. I love the thought of you guys together, but he's hurt you twice. Don't give him the chance to hurt you again."

"I don't think you have to worry about that," Kitty said sadly. "His goodbye sounded final."

"I saw you guys together," Cecily said. "He's mad about you. It's not over, but maybe it should be. You're going to college in a couple of weeks. Maybe it's best to write this summer off as a lesson learned, and move on to someone who treats you better and can appreciate you."

Kitty felt tears filling her eyes again. As Cecily spoke she realized how much she had misjudged her friend. She, like everyone else, had long accused her of being a flighty airhead, but she was a caring person with a lot of depth. Grudgingly, she also admitted that Cecily's words made her unutterably sad. She wanted Dante. She didn't want to start over with some unknown guy at college.

"He treats me well when we're together," Kitty defended. "He just doesn't want to stay together."

"Oh, Kitty," Cecily said, and Kitty could imagine her shaking her head. "You're so far gone over him it's too late, isn't it?"

"Yes," Kitty admitted in a voice barely above a whisper.

"I'm sorry," Cecily said.

"Thanks, Cecily. I miss you."

"I miss you, too. This isn't the summer I had envisioned for us. I wanted to spend tons of time with you before you left for school"

"I know, me too," Kitty said. "But, hey, you can come visit me, and I'll see you when I'm home."

"If I return to Montana," Cecily said.

Kitty's heart turned over in a somersault of fear. She didn't want Cecily to be anywhere but here. She didn't know how much her friend was like her bedrock until the possibility of her absence made her realize it. She needed Cecily, and she needed her to be in Montana like she needed Libby to remain here and take care of their ranch. Was

Dante going to be added to this list of people she needed in order to maintain her equilibrium?

Too late, Cecily's words echoed in her head. *It is too late,* Kitty thought. *I am already too far gone. Somewhere along the way, I fell in love with him.* The thought was so devastating that when she hung up with Cecily, she put her pillow over her face and cried until she fell asleep.

CHAPTER 23

The next morning, Saturday, she woke with puffy eyes and a heavy heart. She stumbled to the bathroom, retrieved a cool cloth, and crawled back in bed.

When she didn't show up for breakfast, Maggie came upstairs to check on her.

"Kitty," she whispered, and knocked tentatively on the door in case she was sleeping.

"Come in," Kitty called. Her nose sounded stuffy from her long night of crying.

"Hey." Maggie poked her head around the door. "Want some company?"

Did she? Always before when something painful occurred she wanted to be left alone. "Yes," she said, and was surprised by how much she meant it. She moved the covers aside, Maggie crawled into her bed, and snuggled down into the blankets.

"Did you guys break up?"

"Yes," Kitty said. She sniffed in an attempt to hold back her tears.

"I'm sorry," Maggie said sincerely. "You want Mathew to beat him up for you?"

Kitty smiled. Not only because the suggestion was funny but

because a few short months ago, she would have wanted that very thing. Funny how quickly life could change.

"No, thanks," she said.

Maggie linked their arms together and rested her head on Kitty's shoulder.

"Did you know Mathew has had a crush on me for most of my life?" she asked.

"Yes. Everyone knew."

Maggie let out a frustrated breath. "That's what he said. Why didn't anyone ever tell me?"

"Because you're innocent. No one wanted you to grow up and have a boyfriend."

"That's not nice. It's not fair to keep me in the dark because people don't want me to grow up."

"I suppose it's not," Kitty said. "But now that I've had a taste of growing up, I can see why we all wanted to keep you from it. Life can be very hard, Maggie. And so can love." She hated the cynical, grownup tone in her voice.

"What's hard about love?" Maggie asked. "You love someone or you don't. It's black and white, as far as I can tell."

Kitty smiled and squeezed Maggie's arm. She hoped it would always be black and white for her sister. Or did she? Her brow puckered. Could anyone appreciate what they had if it came so easily? Maggie and Mathew were undoubtedly sweet together, but how much passion was between them?

"What's it like when you kiss Mathew?" Kitty asked.

Maggie smiled. "It's nice. It's sweet, but also sort of a strange transition. I suppose I'll get used to it. He tells me I will, anyway. I don't think it's weird for him because he's always thought of me this way, but to me he's always been Mathew, the boy next door, you know?"

Kitty squeezed her hand. "I know."

"What was it like to kiss Dante?"

She tried not to wince at the use of the past tense. "It was like what happens when a match touches a firework."

Maggie laughed at Kitty's hyperbolic description.

"No, I mean it. I didn't know it would be like that. I couldn't think. It was like my brain turned off completely. I couldn't form a coherent thought or say an intelligible word."

"Wow," Maggie said before becoming very quiet.

Kitty wondered if she was comparing the two descriptions of kissing. She hoped not, but maybe it wouldn't matter if she did. Maybe Maggie didn't need passion. Maybe her sweet nature couldn't endure it. Maybe the pure and innocent kisses she shared with Mathew would always be enough for her. She hoped so. As for her, she could never go back. Now that she knew what it was to kiss someone so passionately that she had to lean against the wall for support, she could never tolerate anything less. Her chest fluttered with sudden panic. What if she never found it again? What if it was some sort of magic that only came along once in a lifetime? What if Dante was her one chance at passion, and it was gone forever?

"Hang out with me and Mathew today," Maggie said.

"Sure." She might as well. What else did she have to do?

"Really?" Maggie asked. "You never used to want to hang out with us."

That's because I had a huge crush on Mathew, and spending time with you guys was like rubbing a cheese grater over my heart. Kitty smiled ruefully. Life was full of cruel little ironies. Now instead of bringing her pain, spending time with Mathew and Maggie might work as a balm for her wounded heart.

"Where is he?" Kitty asked.

"Downstairs," Maggie said. Her eyes shone with mischief. "Let's bring him up. It will make him squirm with discomfort." She giggled and put her hand over her mouth.

"Margaret Chapman, you're sort of secretly bad, aren't you?"

Maggie nodded. "I learned it by watching my big sisters." She turned toward the door. "Mathew, come up here please."

Kitty supposed she should care that she was in her pajamas, in her bed, and hadn't yet combed her hair or brushed her teeth. She didn't though. As he had said, he was going to be her brother someday. He might as well know what he was in for. Will and Dobbie had both seen her first thing in the morning. It was never too early to begin the family initiation process. Maybe he would appreciate the advanced warning.

Mathew trudged up the stairs and tentatively poked his head around the doorway so only one eye was visible.

"Did you need something, Sweetheart?" he asked.

Maggie patted the bed beside her.

Kitty could read the indecision in his face and had to suppress a laugh. Should he take the opportunity to lie beside the girl of his dreams, or turn tail and run at the sight of her freshly woken sister?

Love won out over fear, and he haltingly stepped into the room.

"Come here," Maggie said, and patted the bed again.

Mathew threw an uncertain look to Kitty. "This is what sisters do," she told him. "Might as well get used to it now."

He gave up and plopped down next to Maggie. He wrapped both arms around her and kissed her cheek.

"This isn't what I envisioned when I thought of us in bed together," he said.

Maggie blushed crimson, but Kitty chuckled. She was shocked to hear Mathew say something so, well, so naughty. He seemed like such a choirboy. Maybe she should keep a more watchful eye on her little sister.

"If my dad ever hears you say anything like that, you'll never walk again," Kitty warned him.

"He's not here, is he?" Mathew asked.

Kitty shook her head. "I'm seeing a whole new side of both of you today."

"That's because you never spend time with us," Maggie said. She clasped Mathew's hand. "But she's going to today."

"Sounds good," Mathew said happily. He was so overjoyed that Maggie was finally aware of him he would have had the same response if she told him they were going to spend the day plucking burrs off a grizzly bear's fur.

"What are we going to do today?" Kitty asked. "What does a day in the life of Maggie and Mathew entail?"

"Once upon a time it was me staring at Maggie while she waded in the creek looking for crawdads, or me staring at Maggie while she checked the barns for new kittens, or me staring at Maggie while she searched the tool shed for baby mice. Now it's mostly the same except occasionally she kisses me."

"Mathew," Maggie said. Kitty didn't have to look at her to know she was blushing. "You stop that. You sound like an obsessed weirdo."

He shook his head. "I'm too rich to be called that. 'Eccentric' is a more accurate description."

Once again Kitty had to hide her shock. She had never heard any of the Henshaws refer to their wealth, especially not so blatantly. She understood now the Mathew she had a crush on for so long was an illusion. The real one was nothing like the boy from her dreams. She liked him, but now her heart was too full of Dante to have any romantic inclinations toward him. He was funny, though.

He sat up and looked around. "Do you have a television in here?"

"No, sorry," Kitty said. "Is there a game on?"

He looked at her with something like pity. "On a Saturday morning? No. I was listening to the news on my way over here, and there's a huge story I wanted to watch."

Kitty sat up now, too. She was something of a news junkie. "What is it?"

"Our state senator was kidnapped," he said. "A group of armed cowboys sneaked into his house in the middle of the night, carried him off, and disappeared with him. Good thing Yancey Blake didn't win. It might have happened to him. Are you all right?"

Kitty had lain down abruptly in the middle of Mathew's story. She suddenly knew what the mystery surrounding Dante's ranch was. *It wouldn't have happened to Yancey Blake,* she thought. *It was Yancey Blake who did it.*

"I'm fine." She sounded anything but fine, even to herself. Her hands were shaking, and her breath was coming out in hollow rasps. Spots appeared before her eyes, and she squeezed them tightly shut. "I'm sorry, but I'm not going to be able to hang out with you guys today."

"Why?" Maggie asked. Kitty was too distracted to feel badly about the disappointment in her tone.

"I have something I need to do," Kitty said.

"What?" Maggie and Mathew asked in unison.

I have to rescue a state senator, and then I have to turn in my boyfriend for kidnapping.

Obviously she couldn't say that. "I'm going to go check on Dante."

"Are you sure?" Maggie asked.

Kitty nodded. "I think he might need me," she said. She swallowed down the lump of panic rising in her throat. First she would help him get out of this mess. Then she would turn him in. Then, if they would let her, she would deck him as hard as she could, right in his smug, handsome face.

athew and Maggie vacated her room, and still she didn't stir from the bed. She had to think. She had to plan, but her brain was sluggish from the shock it had received.

They kidnapped a state senator. What were they thinking? How did they think they would get away with this, and why did they do it? Were they going to kill him? She grimaced, and her stomach turned over. No, she could never believe Dante would be capable of murder. Of course, she wouldn't have thought him capable of kidnapping, and look how that turned out.

She sat up, turned on her laptop, and Googled the phone number for the local FBI office. The phone was in her hand, but she stopped and stared at it. How would she sound, an eighteen year old teenager from the middle of nowhere, calling to say her ex-boyfriend kidnapped the senator? They would laugh her ear off. She would if she were on the other end of the line. After all, she only had a suspicion. What she needed was proof, but how to get it?

There was only one way she could think of, so she stood and started to plan. First things first she had to get ready. She secured her hair in a ponytail and threw on jeans, a t-shirt, and hiking boots. She filled her pockets with anything she thought necessary, and packed a bag with more provisions. When she felt ready, she made herself sit and think—hard. Was there anything else she was missing? Was there anything else she might need?

When she went downstairs, Maggie and Mathew were sitting on the couch. They looked up at her curiously. She knew she wasn't dressed like someone who was about to try and reconcile with her boyfriend.

"If Cecily's home, I might stay over," she said. She knew for a fact that Cecily wasn't home, but she didn't know what she was about to walk into. If for some reason she was out all night, she didn't want her family to worry about her or complicate the situation by looking for her.

"All right," Maggie said. She squinted up at her. "Are you all right, Kitty?"

"Fine," Kitty said. She moved to the door and paused to look back at them. She wanted to warn them somehow, or give them a message, but she couldn't figure out how, so instead she waved and left.

She took a minute to put the contents of her bag into her saddle-bag. It would be less conspicuous than a backpack, and if she was caught, they would surely confiscate her bag anyway.

I can do this, she told herself over and over on the ride to the Blake's ranch. It was a matter of planning and preparation, and she had done her best. All she had to do was sneak onto the ranch, find the proof she was looking for, and sneak back out. An in and out mission. Simple. Piece of cake. Why, then, was her heart beating erratically? Why were her knees weak and knocking against her horse? The poor animal thought she was using her knees to urge him on. He kept springing forward, and he turned to look at her in frustration when she reined him in. The last thing she wanted was to go in with hooves pounding.

She led him to the spot she had used on her previous visit. She tried not to think of how irate Dante had been, or how he warned her never to come back to the ranch. *Of course he didn't want me to visit the ranch. He wanted to keep me in the dark, and he succeeded. Were his kisses a cover? Was he sent to spy on her and her family to find out what they knew?*

She shook her head to clear it. Her suspicions were making her paranoid, and she couldn't afford to be delusional right now. She needed a clear head to complete her mission successfully.

For the third time that summer, she stealthily sneaked onto the Blake's ranch. This time there was no sign of the armed guards she had carefully avoided before. Was it because they were busy guarding the senator?

She was slower today, stealthier. If there was ever a time for caution, it was now. They had already committed a felony by capturing a politician. Would they bat an eyelash over harming a nobody teenager? She doubted it, and that knowledge made her creep slowly along the edge of the pasture. When she reached the far fence she dropped to all fours and waited, watching. There was no activity at all, and that in itself was suspicious. The Chapman's ranch was always busy. Dante had made a joke of that very fact because it seemed they couldn't find a quiet place to make out. But the Blake's spread was quiet, too quiet.

After assuring herself no one was around, she took a deep breath and steeled her spine before ascending the fence. Quickly she darted to the opening of the barn and then froze. Did she hear something, or was it her imagination?

When no sound came after a couple of minutes, she crept forward. There was no one around, she was sure, so it came as a total shock when hands grabbed her and threw her into the hay. She opened her mouth to scream, and then he was kissing her.

Déjà vu, she thought, and then didn't think anything as the kiss exploded her senses. For one brief minute, she didn't care that he had dumped her. She didn't care that he was most likely a criminal who might spend the rest of his life in federal prison. For now, she simply wanted to kiss him and forget anything else. Crazy how easy it was to do. She lost herself totally in his kiss for an unknown length of time. Her fingers stabbed through his hair, drawing him closer.

"Well, what do we have here?" a male voice asked.

Dante immediately broke off the kiss. It took Kitty a while to pull herself out of her fog, but when she did she noticed his eyes were pleading with her.

What, she wanted to say, *what do you want?* But of course she couldn't, so she simply remained quiet.

"What do you mean?" Dante asked the man belligerently. "What do you think it looks like? I'm making out with my girlfriend."

He stood and held out his hand to help Kitty. When she stood, he dropped her hand.

"You know the rules, Blake," the man said. "No trespassers."

"Look, a guy gets lonely; you know what I'm saying?"

Kitty crossed her arms over her chest.

The man didn't respond. He stood stock still, staring at Dante with an icy edge in his eyes. Two more large men with guns joined him to flank his sides, and Kitty started to feel an ominous hole in the pit of her stomach. What had she gotten herself into?

Dante turned to her. "Go home, Kitty." His eyes were so fierce, and so afraid that she didn't dare disobey. She turned to go, but the man's voice stopped her.

"Wait," he said, and held up a hand.

Kitty froze and spun to look at him.

"She doesn't know anything," Dante said. "She's not even from around here. She's from Billings. I met her at a club, and we've been getting together to hook up whenever I'm available. She left her truck parked at the end of the drive and hiked up here to surprise me. Let her go."

The man narrowed his eyes, considering it.

Kitty watched Dante, considering him. Maybe she was crazy, but her only thought was how he could lie with such fluidity. Was that what he had been doing to her all summer? Feeding her lines to keep her happy? Who was he?

The man opened his mouth to speak, and Kitty looked at him. She could tell by his eyes he was going to let her go, and then everything changed.

"Kitty." Yancey Blake entered the barn with another man who was holding a gun. "What are you doing here, honey?"

The man narrowed his eyes at Kitty before turning them on Yancey. "You know this girl?"

"She's our neighbor across the way," Yancey said, and stopped speaking because Dante was furiously shaking his head.

The man looked from Yancey to Kitty to Dante. His eyes bore into Dante, and Kitty started to shake. "Tie her up," he commanded.

Two men advanced on her. Dante took a flying leap and landed on the man who gave the commands.

"Run, Kat," he said. She didn't hesitate to do what he said. Her only usefulness to him would be if she got away.

Unfortunately, she had never been a runner. Despite how hard she tried to get away, two of the men overtook her. They looked unconcerned as they gripped her arms, but if they thought they were going to take her easily, they were in for a surprise.

As if a switch had been flipped, she turned into a furious ball of flying fists and feet. Not for nothing had she lived on a ranch her whole life. She had seen more than one calf successfully get away from the men who were trying to wrangle it, and she used every technique she had ever seen.

For one glorious moment she was free, and then she realized she wasn't the only one who had been struggling.

"Don't you touch my son," Yancey yelled.

Kitty froze in her tracks and turned. Dante was lying on the floor in an unconscious heap. One of the large men turned on Yancey and hit him across the face. Too late she realized her mistake. She tried to take off again, but then one of the men raised the butt of his gun to her head, and everything went black.

CHAPTER 25

Kitty woke slowly, disoriented and uncertain of her surroundings. Her eyes remained closed as she tried to become fully conscious. Her head was pounding and she was certain the moisture she felt caking her hair was blood. Nearby was the sound of someone's steady breathing. Her head rested on something soft, and the warmth indicated it was someone's leg.

Her eyes became slits as she squinted up at her pillow.

"Kat." Dante's voice was tremulous. "I'm so glad to see you awake, sweetheart. How are you?"

"Sore." She sounded raspy. Her throat was dry and painful. She was thirsty. Dim light filtered through a window. "What time is it?"

"I don't know," Dante said. "They took my watch. The sun is setting, so I would guess it's sometime around eight." He used his hands to smooth the hair off her head. She realized his hands were tied at the wrists. When she tried to move her hands she found they were tied, too.

"I've been out a long time," she said. When she arrived at his house, it was around one in the afternoon.

"The longest day of my life. You've lost a lot of blood. We need to get out of here and get you to a doctor."

"I think I'm all right," she said. She felt a lump on the back of her head. She had once read if a lump formed, the injury wasn't usually serious. It was head injuries without lumps that were the real danger.

"But you're all bloody," he said. His eyes were like saucers and filled with worry.

"Head wounds bleed a lot. I think I'm fine." She had a rousing headache, but no blurred or double vision. "Did they frisk me?"

He was puzzled by the question. "Not that I saw."

She smiled. "Thank goodness for the misogynists of Montana."

"If you're using words that big, I know you're all right, although I have no idea what you just said."

"They didn't frisk me because I'm a girl and therefore harmless." She tried to fit her hands in her pocket, but couldn't because they were tied. "Can you reach into my right pocket?"

He raised an eyebrow at her but complied with the request. It took a while to move her off his lap and then arrange himself so he could reach into her pocket.

"Oh, my," he said. He looked at her in wonder. "You brought a knife."

She smiled and tried not to look smug. "This is Montana. Always come prepared." She had brought another important provision, too, but she wouldn't tell him what it was yet. She wasn't sure what his reaction would be.

"I love you," he said flippantly. They froze. "I mean that, Kat. I love you. So much." He leaned in to kiss her, and she let him. This might be their last chance to be together before she discovered a truth that might tear them apart.

When the kiss finished he used the knife to cut the ties holding her hands together. As soon as her hands were free, she took the knife from him and cut his ropes. He pulled her into a tight hug and kissed her again.

"I've never been as afraid in my life as I was when I thought I might lose you," he said.

"What happened? Last thing I remember, I saw you lying unconscious on the floor."

"I wasn't unconscious, I was stunned. They hit me, but didn't knock me out. Of course they almost had to when I opened my eyes and saw that guy hit you with his gun. If I ever get my hands on him…" He trailed off, and his eyes narrowed. "Anyway, they tied us up, blindfolded me, and dropped us here."

"What about your dad?"

"They hit him, too. I don't know what they did with him because they separated us." The worry in his tone was palpable. She pressed her palm to his cheek. He closed his eyes and leaned in to her touch.

She let out a breath and tried to think clearly. It wasn't easy with her pulse throbbing in her ears and her head hurting so much. "We need to get out of here, obviously. They could come back at any time. Do you have any idea where we are?"

He shook his head. "They brought us on horseback, so we're somewhere near the Henshaws' land, our land, or yours."

"That narrows it down," she said wryly. Among the three families there were thousands upon thousands of acres. "How long were we on the horse, do you think?"

He closed his eyes and tried to remember. "Maybe a half hour to forty-five minutes?"

She nodded and looked around. They were in some type of shed. The wood was old and rotting and looked like it had been built a few generations ago. "We don't have any buildings like this on our land, I'm sure of it."

"I don't know if we have any like this on our property. I've never explored all of it."

"I've explored a lot of it, with Cecily, but I don't remember seeing anything like this. Of course, that doesn't mean it doesn't exist. There are lots of places we might have missed. Still, it's likely we're on the Henshaws' land. They have so much they would never check their outbuildings." A sudden thought occurred to her and she lowered her voice to a whisper. "Is there a guard outside?"

"Not that I've heard," he whispered, too. "I heard lots of hooves pounding when they left us here, and no one has checked on us since."

"I'm going to check," she said. She cracked the door and pressed her ear to the opening. When she didn't hear anything she opened it further and poked her head around. "No one. Let's go."

They stepped out of the shack and looked around again. "Now what?" he asked.

"After our last adventure I did some research on how to tell direction."

"I love you," he said again, and he was grinning at her.

She took his hand and squeezed it as she peered up at the sky. "The moon is up already. If the moon rises before midnight it's in the west, so that way is south."

She started to head south, but he stopped her. "Wait, if we're on the Henshaws' property, then your house isn't south of here, it's west. We should go toward the moon."

"All right," she said.

He smiled. "You're going to follow me that easily and without argument?"

"I trust you," she said, and was surprised by her answer. She did trust him, she realized. No matter what his apparent involvement in the kidnapping, she couldn't believe anything bad of him.

He squeezed her hand. "I'm sorry about the breakup, Kat. I wanted to try and spare you involvement in this. I knew you would figure it out, and I thought if you were angry enough, you might stay away when word got out. Guess I should have known your protective instincts would get the better of you."

"Dante, there's something you don't know about me."

"Many things, I bet, but to what are you referring?"

"After Anne left the ranch, Dobbie disappeared for a couple of years to lick his wounds. His absence, along with Anne's, left Dad a little desperate for help. He hired the first guy he found, and it was a huge mistake. Not only did he practically run the ranch into the ground with his ineptitude, but he was a slimy individual. He used to watch me, Maggie, and Libby with an expression that made us all uncomfortable, but he was especially keen on Libby. He started hanging around in the middle of the day to be close to her. Something about him set off my internal alarms, and I started keeping a close eye on him. One day I was in the barn with some new kittens when I heard Maggie screaming bloody murder from the house. I had a good idea of what had happened. The guy found Libby alone in the kitchen, pinned her to the wall and groped her. I grabbed a gun from the cabinet in the barn, loaded it, and went to the house. I held it on him and told him to get out. I'll never forget the way he looked at me. It was a calculating look, like he was deciding whether or not I would actually shoot him. I realized in that moment I would if it meant protecting my sisters. I cocked the gun, and he must have read something in my face that convinced him because he left the house and slunk away before my father could get his hands on him.

"That day changed something within me. I felt as if I had found my calling and started doing some deep thinking about what I want to do with my life. I'm going to Nebraska State because it has one of the best programs in the country for criminal justice. My dream is to someday be in the FBI."

She let the words hang between them. She wasn't sure what his response would be. If he was truly involved in something illegal, he wouldn't be pleased to hear his girlfriend was a future policeman. To her consternation, he started to laugh.

"Oh, Kat, when this is over, we have so much talking to do. And, for the record, I think you're going to be awesome in the FBI. I can totally see you in that capacity, either doing research, or working in the field." He smiled and shook his head. "Life is funny."

She was pleased by his compliment, but irritated she didn't understand his amusement.

"I'll tell you everything," he said. He took her hand and wove their fingers together. "Let's start with us. It's no secret I had a blazing crush on you before I moved away from here."

"I knew," she admitted.

"Of course you did. Everyone knew because I followed you around like a worshipful little puppy hoping for a scrap of your attention. I was a pathetic mess when I was fourteen, and all the years before that. I was short, and shy, and chubby. That summer after we moved, I hit a growth spurt and grew six inches. My baby fat melted away, and I was suddenly taller than most of the guys my age. When I started school in the fall, I looked much the same as I do now, although I'm sure I've filled out and matured some. Anyway, I was determined things were going to be different for me. What I didn't count on was that my physical transformation did nothing to change who I was on the inside. I was still painfully shy and insecure. It took me forever to make friends, and talking to girls was impossible. It still is."

She looked at him in surprise.

He gave her a wry smile. "I know, I made it sound like I'm the voice of experience, but that's because I so badly wanted to impress you with the new me. I thought about you a lot over the years, but I had other crushes on other girls. That day I saw you in our cow pasture, though, it all came rushing back at me. Only now it was more powerful than anything I'd ever experienced. You are the most beautiful, amazing girl I've ever known, Kat. I never wanted anything more than I wanted to be with you the moment I saw you hop the fence. I decided to pursue you, only I would do it the right way. I would be the guy you deserved; the suave and sophisticated guy who knew exactly what he was doing."

"So when you kissed me," she started.

His smile returned, and this time it was shy. "My first kiss, too. I didn't mean to, I promise I didn't, but you were there, and you were so pretty and soft; I couldn't help myself." He paused. "I suppose now that you know the truth about me, you don't want anything to do with me."

Contrary to his words she stopped walking and threw herself into his arms by wrapping her arms around his neck and her legs around his waist. She kissed him soundly for a long minute.

"How could you think I wouldn't like you? You were my friend, and I loved the boy you were."

"But I was," he started, but she cut him off.

"You were sweet and kind and wonderful. You still are, and I love you, Dante. Don't pretend to be anyone else with me. *You* are who I want, the real you, not some Casanova who has all the right moves and lines. Don't you see? We go together perfectly."

"I'm beginning to understand," he murmured between kisses.

Reluctantly she let him go and started walking again. "What's going on with the ranch?"

"You don't know how close I've come to telling you everything on several occasions. I hated keeping secrets from you, Kat, but I had to, for your own protection." He took a deep breath. "At the end of last school year, a couple of FBI agents approached me."

She inhaled sharply.

"See why I was laughing?" he asked. "I know more about the FBI than I want to, believe me. Anyway, they told me my dad had been targeted by a militia. You know Montana is full of them because they can live in the middle of nowhere and remain under the radar. I knew Dad was upset after he lost his senate bid, but I had no idea how demoralized he was until the FBI told me what was going on. They couldn't figure out what this group was planning. You were right when you said it was a strange coincidence I reappeared here in the midst of some very suspicious activity. The FBI asked to use me to spy on my father and the 'Sons of Freedom' group he was now involved with."

"They asked you to spy on your own father?" she asked.

He nodded. "And I was happy to do it. I thought I hated him for what he did to me. I was seething with bitterness and rage over all the wrongs he had committed against me since my birth. But then I showed up here, and he welcomed me with open arms. He was happy to have me back and desperately hoping I would take an interest in the ranch. When he presented me with my Stetson, it was all I could do not to pack my bags and go back to Chicago. And then I started talking to you. When you told me you liked me better when I wasn't angry, it had a profound effect on me, Kat. I want to be the sort of man you deserve, and the last vestiges of my bitterness fell away with that conversation.

"Only that left me in a moral dilemma. Now that I wasn't angry, I had no motivation to spy on my father, and I started to realize some truly nasty things were happening on the ranch. Thank goodness I sent Cecily away in the beginning so she didn't get dragged into this mess."

"Your father's not in charge, is he?"

He shook his head. "He's a pawn. The guy who confronted us in the barn is in charge. I don't know his real name, but everyone calls him Mr. Henry."

"Why?"

"For Patrick Henry. You know, 'Give me liberty, or give me death.' They're radically anti-government as it is now and obsessed with the constitution."

"What's your part in all this?"

"Spying, mostly. I've been reporting their activities to the FBI. When I learned of the kidnapping plot, they wanted to pull me out, but I couldn't leave my dad. I've been trying to talk some sense into him and get him out of this mess, but he wouldn't listen to me. He didn't want me to be involved in it, though. He made me stay at the ranch during the kidnapping and told the others I was going to be on guard."

"Why didn't the FBI stop the kidnapping?"

"I don't know. I thought they were going to, but it's been difficult to contact them. The phones at the ranch are bugged."

"If the phones at your ranch are bugged, how did you..." She trailed off. "Oh. You've been using our phone to contact them." That explained why he came over every day.

"I have, but Kat you've got it all wrong. I only contact them once a week or when some new development happens. I came every day to see you. I've had a great summer with you, even with all the intrigue in my family life."

She nodded, not sure if she believed him. They walked in silence, side by side but not touching until he took her hand and pointed. There, in the distance, was another small outbuilding, and inside they could hear the sound of faint groaning.

CHAPTER 26

"I think that's my dad," Dante whispered. He started to hurry forward, but Kitty held him back.

"We need to sweep the perimeter and make sure no one's around," she said.

He nodded. "How do we do that?"

"I don't know. I heard that term on television, but I don't know what it means."

Even in the midst of his worry, he had to smother a laugh. He leaned close to her ear and whispered. "You're adorable."

She smiled as she scanned the horizon. "I don't see or hear anything. I guess we're safe."

Cautiously they crept forward. The outbuilding wasn't locked, which was strange, Kitty thought, but he was probably tied up and unable to get out. Their captor's mistake had been in stowing them together. Without Dante, she never would have been able to get out on her own.

There was no light in the shack, but they could make out Yancey's still form on the opposite side of the small building.

"Dad." Dante rushed forward and put his hand to his father's head.

Yancey rolled over onto his back. Even in the dim moonlight Kitty could tell his face was bruised and bleeding. "Son?" He used the same croaky tone Kitty had when she first woke up. "Are you all right?"

"I'm fine, Dad. Are you?"

"I will be," Yancey said. Dante helped him sit up and he winced. Kitty handed her knife to Dante, and he cut the ropes off Yancey's hands. "Kitty," he said in astonishment. "Are you all right, honey?"

"I'm fine," she said. She moved to his other side, and together they got him standing.

"Dad-blamed idiots," Yancey muttered. "And I'm the biggest idiot of all for trusting them. I should have my head examined for getting messed up in this business. Guess I'll have plenty of time for that when I'm in prison."

"Let's concentrate on getting out of here," Dante said tightly.

"Don't worry about it," Yancey said, misreading the concern in Dante's tone. "There's no way they can pin anything on you. I made sure of that; you're safe."

"Dad, I know I'm safe. I've been working with the FBI."

Yancey froze and looked at him.

Dante looked away.

"That's why you came back here," Yancey said.

Dante nodded. He looked miserable. Kitty longed to hold him close and ease his hurt.

Yancey blew out a breath. "I suppose I had it coming with the way I treated you."

"Forget about that," Dante said. "It's in the past. I wanted to do the right thing here, but I'm not sure what that is anymore. Spying on my father doesn't feel right."

"It is if the father's a first class idiot who's breaking the law." He shook his head. "Hindsight really is perfect, you know? When I met these men, we seemed to be on the same page. I didn't see how they were using me and leading me down a blind alley until it was too late. There's no fool worse than an old fool."

"You're not a fool, Mr. Blake, you're a passionate man who wants things to change. Lots of people have felt frustrated with our government lately."

"I appreciate that, sweetie," he said in the gentle tone she remembered. "But I have no one to blame for the mess I've made but myself. Your mother was right to leave me." He turned to Dante.

"She would say so, too, if she could hear you feeling sorry for yourself this way," Dante said. Kitty was about to chastise him for his harshness, but it worked because Yancey laughed and seemed to perk up in their grasp. "True enough she would. I bet she's going to love telling me what kind of fool I've been."

"She loves you," Dante said.

Kitty couldn't tell for sure, but she wondered if the sudden heat emanating from Yancey was a blush. "Does she now?"

"I've seen it with my own eyes," Kitty volunteered.

"You saw Shelby?" Yancey asked.

"When I went to Chicago with Dante," Kitty said.

"You went to Chicago with Dante?" He turned to his son. "You're a fine one for keeping secrets."

"Isn't he, though," Kitty muttered.

"Let's concentrate on the problem at hand," Dante said uncomfortably.

"What is going on with you two?" Yancey asked.

When neither Kitty nor Dante answered, he tried again.

"I thought you said you were seeing a stranger you met in Billings," Yancey said. "And she was staying with the Chapmans."

"You said what?" Kitty exploded. Now it made sense why Yancey had said "that girl" so derisively. She remembered her hurt when she thought he was talking about her.

"I didn't want to tell you I was seeing Kitty. I wasn't sure if I could trust you, and I didn't want her involved in what was going on over here."

Yancey fumed inwardly for a minute before softening. He chuckled. "You two. That's sort of a dream come true, I guess."

"For me, too," Dante said. He covered Kitty's hand where it rested on Yancey's back.

"You Blakes are going to turn my head," Kitty said.

"Nah, you're too sensible for that," Yancey said. "I bet Shelby and Cecily fell all over themselves in delight when they found out."

"They did," Dante said.

Kitty smiled. Her family hadn't said so, but she knew they were pleased about her and Dante, too. The dread of all their lives was that one of them would become involved with a stranger who would disrupt the happy harmony of their home. So far, Anne was the only one who fell for an outsider, but they all loved Will, and he loved them in return.

"You're going to have some making up to do with my family," Kitty told Dante. "They're not happy you dumped me again, and neither is Cecily. Maggie wanted to send Mathew to beat you up."

"I'd like to see him try," Dante said. "Although, I'm sure you would love nothing more than seeing your precious Mathew thrash me about." His jealousy was unmistakable, and Kitty smiled again.

"He's not precious to me, but it would be interesting to see which one of you would win a fight."

"Kat, you're always supposed to think I will win the fight, no matter who I'm up against. It's part of being my girlfriend. And what do you mean he's not precious to you? I know how you feel about him."

Kitty felt awkward having this discussion in front of Yancey, but he had either tuned them out or was pretending to. "Mathew is Maggie's boyfriend."

"And he's off limits to you. I get it."

"No, you don't. I don't want Mathew. Maybe I had a little crush on him for a while, but it's nothing compared to what I feel for you."

"And what do you feel for me? I forget."

She could tell he was smiling. She grasped his hand on Yancey's back and squeezed his fingers until it became painful.

"Oh, now I remember," he said. He removed his hand from her clutch and flexed his fingers. "Why couldn't I have fallen for some wimpy Chicago girl who most likely wouldn't beat me in an arm-wrestling match? Montana girls are dangerous."

"You have no idea," Kitty said. She thought with some satisfaction about the things he still didn't know about her. It would be fun to reveal her secrets to him, and she amused herself by thinking of the best way to clue him in on her favorite hobby. Little did she know he was about to get a front row seat.

"Well this is a happy little reunion," said a hauntingly familiar voice. In front of them, Mr. Henry stepped into the moonlight. Kitty could barely make out his form, but there was no mistaking the glint of metal in his hands, or the barrel of the gun that was pointed right at her.

CHAPTER 27

"What are you doing out here, Henry?" Yancey asked. He wrenched free of Dante and Kitty's assistance and gasped with the pain the effort cost him.

"That's *Mr.* Henry to you, Mr. Blake. Let's maintain proper manners," the man said.

He's crazy, Kitty thought. There was no rationalizing with someone who wasn't rational. She began to make her own plans. Mr. Henry turned the gun from her to Dante and Yancey. *That's right*, she thought. *I'm a harmless girl. Ignore me.* His failure to consider her a threat might save them all. Slowly, and while his attention was diverted, she started to creep away, inch by inch.

Dante caught her eye. She tried to convey to him silently what she was planning, but of course he didn't understand her. All he knew was that she might escape, and that was what he wanted most.

"Where's Mason?" he asked, and Mr. Henry's attention turned to him. Mason was the state senator they captured.

"Oh, that's all over now. Turns out someone tipped off the FBI. Mason was wired, and they were following us the whole time. The man's ineptitude is costing the future of this country, and now he's going to be hailed as a hero for taking part in his own kidnapping." He shook his head. "What is this country coming to? Anyway, the law descended on us in droves. There was a little shootout, and I escaped."

"To come take care of the witnesses you left behind," Yancey said. He, too, was moving slowly, only he wasn't moving away from Mr. Henry, he was moving toward him.

"Something like that," Mr. Henry said. "Although, I would prefer if we do this quickly. Too many people know we left you in those shacks and I don't trust them not to confess everything. Good help is hard to find these days, don't you think?"

"I thought you believed in making this country a better place, but you're nothing more than a kidnapper and a murderer," Yancey said. He took another small step forward.

"That's far enough," Mr. Henry said. "I don't answer to you, Mr. Blake, but surely you must realize that true sacrifice has never been accomplished without a little bloodshed. The framers of our constitution knew that. It's why we had a revolution."

"You're sick," Yancey said.

The tension between the men was now so high Mr. Henry had forgotten about Kitty completely. She edged around the circle of their standoff until she was behind Mr. Henry, and then everything happened at once.

"That's far enough, I said," Mr. Henry said. He raised his gun level with Yancey's head.

"Dad, stop," Dante said.

"Someone has to stop you," Yancey said. He took another step. Mr. Henry placed his finger on the trigger and prepared to squeeze. Dante leapt to tackle his father. Kitty sensed her opportunity and stepped forward. She withdrew her gun from the waistband of her pants, released the safety, and pressed it into Mr. Henry's shoulder.

"Everyone stop," she said levelly.

Something in her cool tone forced the three men to freeze. Dante was on top of Yancey and pinning him to the ground. Mr. Henry still had his weapon trained on them.

"Slowly and carefully give me your gun," Kitty said. "One false move, and I won't hesitate to use mine."

Dante and Yancey were looking at her with equally shocked expressions. Dante's mouth hung open so far he resembled a wind tunnel.

Mr. Henry chuckled. "Those are big words from a little girl, honey, but you don't have what it takes to shoot a man."

"Don't test your theory," Kitty said, although she wondered if what he said was true. There was a difference between target practice and holding her gun pressed into another human's flesh. Could she really shoot him?

Then he did something that made her decision easy. He pointed his gun at Dante, and she knew he was going to fire. She steadied her hand and pulled the trigger. He dropped to the ground in a howl of pain, and she stooped to retrieve the gun from his now limp fingers.

"Mr. Blake, are we on the Henshaws' property?" she asked.

He didn't answer. He and Dante were still frozen in place, staring at her in wonder.

"Mr. Blake," she prompted.

"Uh, yeah, this is the Henshaws'," he said at last.

"Dante, do you have your phone on you?" she asked. She had to repeat it again with more urgency because he was also still staring at her in shell-shocked silence.

"Yes," he said at last. Then his brain finally began to work, and he took it out. "I didn't think about that." He opened the phone and dialed.

The Henshaws were the only people for miles who had a cellular tower. Their property was the only place a cell phone would work. Kitty knelt, ripped Mr. Henry's shirt and used a wad of it to staunch his bleeding.

"Is he going to die?" Dante asked.

Kitty shook her head. "I shot him in the right shoulder and I was careful to miss all the major arteries. In fact, we shouldn't trust that he won't try something when he gets over the shock." She handed her gun to Yancey. "Keep this on him while I try and stop the bleeding."

"You shot me," Mr. Henry said hoarsely as he looked up into Kitty's eyes. "I can't believe I got shot by a girl."

"Obviously you've never been married," Yancey said dryly.

Dante spoke into the phone and remained on the line while the FBI used GPS to pinpoint their location.

He covered the mouthpiece. "They're in the woods looking for him already. They'll be here any minute."

Mr. Henry groaned.

"Hush up, you," Yancey said menacingly. "Or else I might get in a few licks before they get here."

The FBI entered the clearing with guns held aloft. Yancey slowly raised his hands. One of the agents confiscated Kitty's gun from him and put him in handcuffs. Another agent took over Kitty's first aid duties while a third agent ushered her and Dante out of the woods.

When they exited the forest, the scene was a madhouse. Law enforcement vehicles of every sort were there with lights blazing, including the sheriff, state patrol, and a dozen unmarked black vehicles she assumed belonged to the FBI. There were two ambulances and two fire trucks. As soon as it was clear they were the victims and not suspects, emergency personnel descended on them in a mass.

"Let's get her to the hospital," one of the FBI agents said. He attempted to hand her over to a paramedic, but she refused.

"I'm fine," she said.

"Honey, have you seen yourself," the paramedic said. "You don't look fine."

Dante stepped forward with a frown. He put his arm around Kitty, and she hid her amusement by burying her face in his chest. The paramedic was young and nice looking.

"If my girlfriend says she's fine, then she's fine," he said.

The paramedic shrugged and walked off.

"You really should go to the hospital," Dante said. He turned and put both arms around her.

"You said I was fine," she reminded him.

"I didn't want that guy's hands on you. Doesn't mean I think you don't need some medical attention. Your head might need stitches."

She shook her head and winced with the effort. "The bleeding has stopped. It's a little cut and a knot. I'm fine, really."

He kissed her forehead. "Let's agree not to have any more adventures for a while, all right?"

She nodded, and then winced again. "I wouldn't mind some aspirin."

One of the FBI agents overheard her. "Can I get some pain reliever for the lady?" He looked around, but everyone looked at each other in confusion. Apparently law enforcement types didn't typically carry pain reliever while they were on duty.

"Did you, by any chance, find my horse?" she asked the man.

He perked up. "We did find a horse tied to a tree not too far from here. We didn't know who it belonged to, so we left it here until we figured it out." He looked behind him and called over his shoulder. "Bring the horse."

Yet another agent led her horse forward. He looked comical wearing a three-piece dark suit and leading her gently loping horse.

"Hey, Flicka," she said. Her horse gave a happy snuffle and nibbled the palm of her hand. She patted its nose and opened her saddlebag. "Here." She tossed a bottle of water to Dante along with a sack lunch she had prepared for him. She fished around until she found her bottle of pain reliever and took it along with a giant swig of water.

She and Dante sat, ate, and drank in silence. She hadn't eaten or had anything to drink in about twelve hours, and she knew the same was probably true for Dante. Exhaustion was creeping in. She began to wonder if they had been forgotten in the swirl of activity.

"Do you think it would be all right if we went home?" she asked.

"I don't think my home is livable right now," he said sadly.

She set aside her meal, crawled into his lap, and secured her arms tightly around his neck. "I'm sorry." She buried her face in his neck. "Stay with us until you go back to school."

"There's nowhere I would rather be," he said sincerely. He ran a soothing hand down her back. "I'm sorry I got you into this mess, Kat."

"You didn't get me into anything," she assured him. "I got myself into it."

"And got us out of it. I can't believe you were hiding a gun that whole time." He shook his head. "Sometimes it's like I don't know you at all."

She smiled against his neck and then smiled wider when she felt his pulse quicken. "You know me better than anyone. There are a couple of details you're lacking, such as the fact that I love guns. Dad bought me that gun for my eighteenth birthday. I'm a champion skeet shooter, and I love target practice."

"When did that start? I'm sure I would have remembered that about you."

"It started after the event with the foreman. I realized if I wanted a career in law enforcement I would have to become comfortable with guns. I started shooting out of a practical desire to get acquainted with them, but then it turned into a passionate hobby. Dad thinks it's a hoot. We go shooting together a lot, although I only shoot targets. I'm not a hunter."

His arms tightened. "All the girls in the world, and I'm stuck with a sharp-shooting cowgirl from Montana," he said affectionately.

"That's the second time you said you're stuck with me."

"Of course I am. There's no one in the world for me besides you. I can never get away from you. The good news is I don't want to. I love you, Kat."

He kissed her then, but it was brief because they were soon interrupted by someone clearing his throat.

CHAPTER 28

"Sorry to have left you alone for so long, but it doesn't seem like you minded much," the agent said wryly. "I need to get a statement from each of you. Is there somewhere more comfortable we can go?"

"We can go to my house," Kitty said. She and Dante sat cuddled together next to the agent who chattered inanely about the beauty of Montana on the ride to her house.

When they pulled up in front of her house, she knew she was in trouble.

"Uh-oh," she said. All the lights were blazing, and their ranch hands were tearing around the yard in a frenzy. Everything came to a stand still when she and Dante emerged from the truck.

Her father strode out onto the porch looking for all the world like Zeus come to life and ready to throw down thunder.

"Where in tarnation have you been young lady?" he yelled. Kitty knew him well enough to hear the worry that colored his angry words. He looked behind her. "It's all right, boys, you can go to bed now, the search is off. Thank you. Sleep in tomorrow if you can."

The hands nodded and mumbled before turning and heading back to the bunkhouse.

"Well?" Her father crossed his arms over his chest.

"Dad, maybe it would be best if we went inside," Kitty said.

For the first time, he seemed to notice Dante and the FBI agent along with the black SUV.

"That's so," he said. He turned and led the way inside.

In the kitchen Maggie was crying while Mathew tried to comfort her. Libby was attempting to make coffee with shaking hands until Dobbie took over and gently removed the implements from her fingers.

"I'll do it, honey," he said.

"She's here," Matt Chapman announced. Everyone spun to look at her. Maggie's weeping increased, and Libby burst into tears before collapsing into Dobbie's arms.

"Sorry I scared you," Kitty said penitently.

"It was my fault," Dante said. He stepped up and put an arm around Kitty.

"It was neither of their faults," the FBI agent said.

"Let's hear it," Mathew said. He offered the man a chair, and they all sat at the large kitchen table.

"Dante has been working with us for a few months now reporting on the activities of the militia living on his ranch," the FBI man said. Kitty learned his name was Reames. She had no idea of his first name because he didn't give it. "I'm not sure how your daughter came to be involved. I'm curious about that myself. Why don't you start from the beginning, and tell us what happened today?" He set out a recording device and pressed the on button.

Dante took a breath. "Last night, the men who have been staying with us kidnapped state senator Mason."

There was a collective gasp around the room.

"I knew it," Matt exclaimed. "I knew they were up to no good over there."

"Kitty figured it out and came to the ranch to check on me today," he continued.

"You did what?" her father raged.

"You told me to tell you if anything was going on, but I needed proof before I said anything."

Matt put his hands to his head. "What kind of fool notion gave you the idea I wanted you to put yourself in that sort of danger? I meant tell me if you heard anything, not go traipsing into the middle of a kidnapping and get yourself hurt."

Kitty blinked at him until he calmed down, and then Dante continued. "Anyway, the men caught her sneaking in. I tried to pass it off as a tryst." His face colored uncomfortably when Matt's eyes narrowed at him. "But they didn't buy it. When they put their hands on her, she fought them, so they knocked her out." His fists clenched and he swallowed hard. "That's how she got this." He gingerly touched the knot at the top of Kitty's head.

"Oh, my poor baby," Libby said. She jumped up and bustled about to make an ice pack for Kitty. Then she remained standing to pour coffee and set out a tray of cookies.

"They put us in a little shack on your property." He nodded to Mathew. "When she came to, I discovered she had a knife in her pocket." He paused to give Kitty an approving smile. "We cut ourselves free and left. We stumbled upon Dad in another building a while later. Not long after that, Mr. Henry found us."

"Who's Mr. Henry?" Dobbie asked. He took a cookie off the tray and nibbled mindlessly.

"He's the leader of the militia," Agent Reames inserted. "This is the part I'm most curious about. What happened next?" He turned his attention back to Dante.

Dante shook his head. "This is the part I still can't believe. Kitty sneaked away while Dad and Mr. Henry were arguing. She got the drop on him and shoved a gun in his back."

Libby gasped and buried her head in Dobbie's shoulder as if the mental image were too much for her.

"Cool as a cucumber she told him to hand over his gun, but of course he didn't. He aimed his gun at me, so she shot him in the shoulder."

For a moment, everyone sat around looking at Kitty until the silence became uncomfortable. She squirmed under their intense scrutiny. Even Agent Reames, who thought he had seen it all, was stunned into speechlessness.

"She wants to be in the FBI," Dante told him.

The shocked silence around the table increased. He forgot she had never told anyone else what she wanted to do with her life.

"Remind me to give her a letter of recommendation for her file," Agent Reames murmured.

"I would appreciate that," Kitty said. Her level tone made everyone smile because it was so much like her to calmly shoot a man and then ask for a letter of recommendation for her file.

They replayed the events of the night a few times, filling in details as the questions came. The rest of the family went to bed a few hours later. Agent Reames stayed while Dante and Kitty wrote formal statements.

"What's going to happen to my dad?" Dante asked.

"I can't say for sure," Agent Reames said.

"He didn't know what he was getting into," Dante said. "He tried to protect me in the barn."

"And he tried to protect both of us at the end. He was going to take on Mr. Henry," Kitty added. Dante clasped her hand, and she squeezed his reassuringly.

"I'll let the prosecutor know. That may earn some leniency for him as well as your helpfulness and involvement in the case. If we're lucky, the prosecutor may view your father as a hapless victim caught up in something he couldn't control."

"And if not," Dante said. "What's the worst case scenario?"

Agent Reames expelled a sigh. "Worst case scenario is that he'll be charged with kidnapping. There's the possibility of life in prison. From what I know of the prosecutor, I would guess he'll come in somewhere in between with a conspiracy to commit kidnapping charge. It's serious, but not as serious, and your father will be out of prison in less than a decade."

Dante sat back, stunned. "A decade."

Agent Reames clapped him on the shoulder. "I know that seems bad, son, but it could be much worse. One of our agents was shot by their men. This militia group is serious and deadly. Most of them won't see the light of day again outside a prison. Believe me when I tell you that if your father gets a decade, he'll be getting off lightly."

Dante nodded, but the pain didn't leave his eyes.

The agent collected their statements and snapped shut his briefcase. "I'll be in touch soon. You're both going to have to testify, unless they confess and skip a trial. You never know with these militia types." He nodded and said goodbye before exiting the house.

They were quiet until they heard his engine start, and then Dante turned to her with sorrow etched on his face.

"What have I done?" He put his hands over his eyes and shuddered with the effort it took not to cry.

"Come on, let's go into the living room," Kitty said. She held out her hand for Dante and led him to the couch. He sank wearily into it. She covered him with an afghan before sitting down beside him and snuggling into his embrace.

"None of this is your fault, Dante, you know that."

"I don't feel that way. I feel like I've singlehandedly ruined my father and destroyed our home."

She looked up at him and smoothed her hand over his forehead. "If anything you saved him. You heard what Agent Reames said. Because of your involvement he's going to request leniency for your father. Because you were here, your dad turned against those men and tried to protect you. If not for you, he might spend the rest of his life in prison."

"Because of me, he's only going to spend a decade there," he said bitterly.

"That's right," Kitty said. "Your father understands that he brought this on himself. He doesn't blame you."

"That doesn't absolve me of my part in it," he said.

"I know it's painful, Dante, but you did the right thing. You might have saved Senator Mason's life. If you hadn't tipped off the FBI about the kidnapping, who knows what they would have done to him? They were prepared to kill us, how much worse would it have been for the man they blamed for ruining the government? I'm proud of you," she said earnestly. "You're the sort of man I want my son to be. Our son," she added shyly. She traced a pattern over his shirt.

He swallowed convulsively. His heart rhythm increased until it matched the frantic beating of her heart. "It's not going to be easy to be apart when we return to school."

"It's only two years," she said. "If you can't get a job near Omaha when you graduate, then I'll transfer to be near you."

"Are you sure, Kat? Are you sure you want me? You could have anyone."

She smiled at his delusional assessment. He saw her differently than she saw herself, that was for sure. "I want you. Only you. Always."

"It's strange how the best night of my life is also the worst night of my life, but you're right; we'll make it work. I love you, Kat." He leaned down to kiss her. He meant for it to be a tender, gentle kiss, but when their lips met, something erupted between them, and they kissed passionately for a long moment.

"Like a match to a firework," she murmured.

"What?" he asked.

"Nothing," she said. She rested her head on his chest. He leaned his head on hers, and a few minutes later, they were asleep.

*A*s it happened, the only trial at which Dante and Kitty had to testify at was the one for Yancey Blake, but they testified in his defense. The other militiamen had refused to speak. They issued a joint statement saying that under the original constitution they were innocent, but the justice system had become so corrupt they decided to plead guilty and spare everyone the mockery of a rigged trial.

Despite the earnest pleading of both Kitty and Dante, Yancey was found guilty of conspiracy to commit kidnapping. He was sentenced to a decade in federal prison with the possibility of parole after five years. Their only consolation was that he was being sent to a medium security facility filled with mostly white-collar criminals. After his initial adjustment, he seemed at peace with prison life. Best of all, he and Shelby had renewed their affection for each other. She was still living in Chicago, but only because she had a steady job with a good income.

Dante offered to drop out of college to help run the ranch and also to help with expenses because the trial had been costly. His mother put her foot down by pointing out he was soon going to become an actuary, which was a high-paying job.

"You'll be able to help more financially once you have a steady income," she said. Since she was remaining at her job for the same reason, he couldn't argue with her logic.

To everyone's surprise, Cecily stepped up to take over the reins of her family's ranch. She didn't yet know what she was doing, but she was learning more every day. She had a natural aptitude, despite her lack of training.

For a while, their community was in the news and on television due to the national coverage the trial received. Kitty managed to stay out of the papers, but there were a few pictures of her home and family that filtered their way into the media.

Yancey's trial took place the summer following the kidnapping, and the notoriety of the area brought tourists who gawked at their ranch as well as the Blakes' ranch. At the same time a few new ranch hands came seeking work, and Kitty was suspicious of their motivation.

"Don't you find it odd they happened to show up here looking for work when our families are so much in the news?" she asked Dante one evening. He was living at the ranch for the summer to help Cecily try to get it in order.

"No, Kat, I don't. I think maybe you're a little paranoid from all the publicity."

"Maybe so," she admitted. But there was one cowboy in particular who unnerved her. His name was Steve, and he first came to their ranch seeking work. Her father sent him away because they didn't need any extra help.

"You might try the Henshaws," Matt Chapman said. "They're always looking for laborers."

The man nodded and started to go, but then he stopped and fastened his gaze on Maggie who had just rounded the barn. What Kitty saw in his expression chilled her. It was a strange sort of recognition, as if he had found something he had been missing. When she heard later that he got the job with the Henshaws, her uncomfortable feeling increased.

"Maggie, have you met that new cowboy the Henshaws hired?"

"Yes," Maggie said. "He introduced himself to me." She smiled. "I think it made Mathew jealous. He's sort of cute."

"I don't like him."

Maggie looked at her in surprise. "Do you know him?"

Kitty shook her head.

"That's not nice, Kitty," Maggie chastised. "He's probably another lonely cowboy."

"All the same, I want you to warn Mathew to keep an eye on him," Kitty said.

"I can't do that. I never talk to Mathew about business, let alone tell him how to run it. Besides, he hardly does anything at the ranch. His Dad and Marcus are in charge of everything. They treat Mathew like a baby." She puckered her sweet face into a frown. *Just like everyone here treats me*, she thought, but didn't say it.

Kitty let out an exasperated breath. If Maggie wouldn't cooperate then she would circumvent her and talk to Mathew herself. Something didn't feel right about the new cowboy. A year ago, she would have chucked her bad feeling up to an overactive imagination, but since her experience with the militia she didn't ignore her gut feelings. Above all, she had to keep her family safe.

"If you feel that strongly about it I'll talk to Mr. Henshaw with you," Dante said when she broached the subject with him.

"You would do that, even though you don't agree with me?" she asked.

"Of course I would." He cupped his hands on her face. "Your happiness and well-being mean more to me than anything."

"Have I told you lately that I love you, Dante?"

"Yes, but it's not nearly enough. Tell me again."

"Let me show you." She stood on her toes to kiss him, and the rest of the world faded away.

*T*hank you for reading *Cowgirl Undercover*, book 3 in the Queens of Montana series. For more books, please visit my website at www.vanessagraybartal.com